APR   2014

JUST SO STORIES

For Little Children

VOLUME II

RUDYARD KIPLING

ILLUSTRATED BY

IAN WALLACE

GROUNDWOOD BOOKS
HOUSE OF ANANSI PRESS
TORONTO   BERKELEY

First published as *Just So Stories*, written and illustrated by Rudyard
Kipling in London in 1902 by Macmillan and Co. Ltd.
This re-illustrated edition published in Canada and the USA in 2014
by Groundwood Books
Illustrations copyright © 2014 by Ian Wallace

Groundwood Books / House of Anansi Press
110 Spadina Avenue, Suite 801, Toronto, Ontario M5V 2K4
or c/o Publishers Group West
1700 Fourth Street, Berkeley, CA 94710

We acknowledge for their financial support of our publishing program
the Canada Council for the Arts, the Government of Canada through
the Canada Book Fund (CBF) and the Ontario Arts Council.

Library and Archives Canada Cataloguing in Publication
Kipling, Rudyard, 1865-1936, author
Just so stories : for little children / written by Rudyard Kipling ;
illustrated by Ian Wallace.
Originally published in 1902.
Issued in print and electronic formats.
ISBN 978-1-55498-213-4 (bound : v. 2).—ISBN 978-1-55498-215-8
(html : v. 2)
1. Animals — Juvenile fiction. I. Wallace, Ian, illustrator II. Title.
PR4854.J85 2013   j823'.8   C2013-900874-8
C2013-900875-6

Design by Michael Solomon
The illustrations were done in watercolour, pencil crayon,
pastel pencil and chalk.
Printed and bound in Singapore

To Patsy

I W

Contents

•

THE BEGINNING OF
THE ARMADILLOES

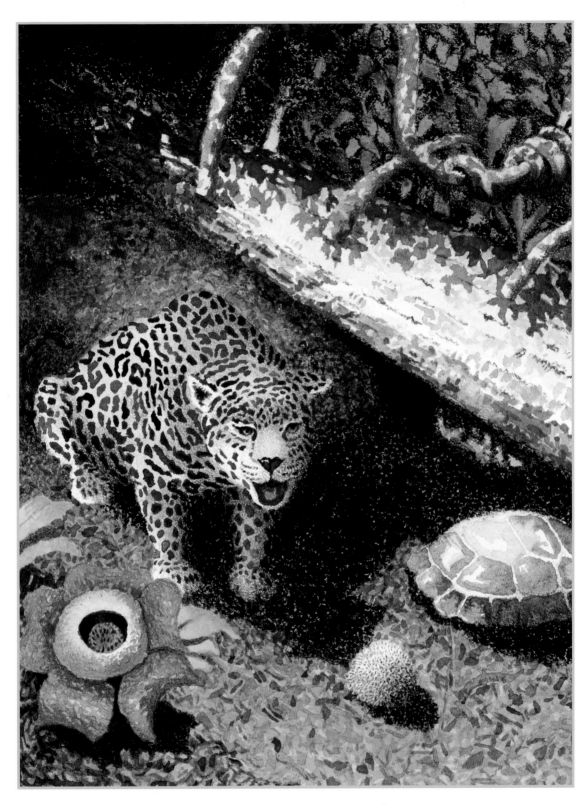

"Now attend to me," said Painted Jaguar.

THIS, O BEST BELOVED, is another story of the High and Far-Off Times. In the very middle of those times was a Stickly-Prickly Hedgehog, and he lived on the banks of the turbid Amazon, eating shelly snails and things. And he had a friend, a Slow-Solid Tortoise, who lived on the banks of the turbid Amazon, eating green lettuces and things. And so *that* was all right, Best Beloved. Do you see?

But also, and at the same time, in those High and Far-Off Times, there was a Painted Jaguar, and he lived on the banks of the turbid Amazon too; and he ate everything that he could catch. When he could not catch deer or monkeys he would eat frogs and beetles; and when he could not catch frogs and beetles he went to his Mother Jaguar, and she told him how to eat hedgehogs and tortoises.

She said to him ever so many times, graciously waving her tail, "My son, when you find a Hedgehog you must drop him into the water and then he will uncoil, and when you catch a Tortoise you must scoop him out of his shell with your paw." And so that was all right, Best Beloved.

One beautiful night on the banks of the turbid Amazon,

Painted Jaguar found Stickly-Prickly Hedgehog and Slow-and-Solid Tortoise sitting under the trunk of a fallen tree. They could not run away, and so Stickly-Prickly curled himself up into a ball, because he was a Hedgehog, and Slow-and-Solid Tortoise drew in his head and feet into his shell as far as they would go, because he was a Tortoise; and so *that* was all right, Best Beloved. Do you see?

"Now attend to me," said Painted Jaguar, "because this is very important. My mother said that when I meet a Hedgehog I am to drop him into the water and then he will uncoil, and when I meet a Tortoise I am to scoop him out of his shell with my paw. Now which of you is Hedgehog and which is Tortoise? because, to save my spots, I can't tell."

"Are you sure of what your Mummy told you?" said Stickly-Prickly Hedgehog. "Are you quite sure? Perhaps she said that when you uncoil a Tortoise you must shell him out of the water with a scoop, and when you paw a Hedgehog you must drop him on the shell."

"Are you sure of what your Mummy told you?" said Slow-and-Solid Tortoise. "Are you quite sure? Perhaps she said that when you water a Hedgehog you must drop him into your paw, and when you meet a Tortoise you must shell him till he uncoils."

"I don't think it was at all like that," said Painted Jaguar, but he felt a little puzzled; "but, please, say it again more distinctly."

"When you scoop water with your paw you uncoil it with a Hedgehog," said Stickly-Prickly. "Remember that, because it's important."

"*But,*" said the Tortoise, "when you paw your meat you drop it into a Tortoise with a scoop. Why can't you understand?"

"You are making my spots ache," said Painted Jaguar; "and besides, I didn't want your advice at all. I only wanted to know which of you is Hedgehog and which is Tortoise."

"I shan't tell you," said Stickly-Prickly. "But you can scoop me out of my shell if you like."

"Aha!" said Painted Jaguar. "Now I know you're Tortoise. You thought I wouldn't! Now I will." Painted Jaguar darted out his paddy-paw just as Stickly-Prickly curled himself up, and of course Jaguar's paddy-paw was just filled with prickles. Worse than that, he knocked Stickly-Prickly away and away into the woods and the bushes, where it was too dark to find him. Then he put his paddy-paw into his mouth, and of course the prickles hurt him worse than ever. As soon as he could speak he said, "Now I know he isn't Tortoise at all. But" — and then he scratched his head with his un-prickly paw — "how do I know that this other is Tortoise?"

"But I *am* Tortoise," said Slow-and-Solid. "Your mother was quite right. She said that you were to scoop me out of my shell with your paw. Begin."

"You didn't say she said that a minute ago," said Painted

Jaguar, sucking the prickles out of his paddy-paw. "You said she said something quite different."

"Well, suppose you say that I said that she said something quite different, I don't see that it makes any difference; because if she said what you said I said she said, it's just the same as if I said what she said she said. On the other hand, if you think she said that you were to uncoil me with a scoop, instead of pawing me into drops with a shell, I can't help that, can I?"

"But you said you wanted to be scooped out of your shell with my paw," said Painted Jaguar.

"If you'll think again you'll find that I didn't say anything of the kind. I said that your mother said that you were to scoop me out of my shell," said Slow-and-Solid.

"What will happen if I do?" said the Jaguar most sniffily and most cautious.

"I don't know, because I've never been scooped out of my shell before; but I tell you truly, if you want to see me swim away you've only got to drop me into the water."

"I don't believe it," said Painted Jaguar. "You've mixed up all the things my mother told me to do with the things that you asked me whether I was sure that she didn't say, till I don't know whether I'm on my head or my painted tail; and now you come and tell me something I *can* understand, and it makes me more mixy than before. My mother told me that I was to drop one of you two into the water, and as you seem so anxious to be dropped I think you don't want to be dropped. So jump into the turbid Amazon and be quick about it."

"I warn you that your Mummy won't be pleased. Don't tell her I didn't tell you," said Slow-and-Solid.

"If you say another word about what my mother said — " the Jaguar answered, but he had not finished the sentence before Slow-and-Solid quietly dived into the turbid Amazon, swam under water for a long way, and came out on the bank where Stickly-Prickly was waiting for him.

"That was a very narrow escape," said Stickly-Prickly. "I don't like Painted Jaguar. What did you tell him that you were?"

"I told him truthfully that I was a truthful Tortoise, but he wouldn't believe it, and he made me jump into the river to see if I was, and I was, and he is surprised. Now he's gone to tell his Mummy. Listen to him!"

They could hear Painted Jaguar roaring up and down among the trees and the bushes by the side of the turbid Amazon, till his Mummy came.

"Son, son!" said his mother ever so many times, graciously waving her tail, "what have you been doing that you shouldn't have done?"

"I tried to scoop something that said it wanted to be scooped out of its shell with my paw, and my paw is full of per-ickles," said Painted Jaguar.

"Son, son!" said his mother ever so many times, graciously waving her tail, "by the prickles in your paddy-paw

*"Son, son! What have you been doing that
you shouldn't have done?"*

I see that that must have been a Hedgehog. You should have dropped him into the water."

"I did that to the other thing; and he said he was a Tortoise, and I didn't believe him, and it was quite true, and he has dived under the turbid Amazon, and he won't come up again, and I haven't anything at all to eat, and I think we had better find lodgings somewhere else. They are too clever on the turbid Amazon for poor me!"

"Son, son!" said his mother ever so many times, graciously waving her tail, "now attend to me and remember what I say. A Hedgehog curls himself up into a ball and his prickles stick out every which way at once. By this you may know the Hedgehog."

"I don't like this old lady one little bit," said Stickly-Prickly, under the shadow of a large leaf. "I wonder what else she knows?"

"A Tortoise can't curl himself up," Mother Jaguar went on, ever so many times, graciously waving her tail. "He only draws his head and legs into his shell. By this you may know the Tortoise."

"I don't like this old lady at all — at all," said Slow-and-Solid Tortoise. "Even Painted Jaguar can't forget those directions. It's a great pity that you can't swim, Stickly-Prickly."

"Don't talk to me," said Stickly-Prickly. "Just think how much better it would be if you could curl up. This *is* a mess! Listen to Painted Jaguar."

Painted Jaguar was sitting on the banks of the turbid Amazon sucking prickles out of his paw and saying to himself: —

"Can't curl, but can swim —
Slow-Solid, that's him!
Curls up, but can't swim —
Stickly-Prickly, that's him!"

"He'll never forget that this month of Sundays," said Stickly-Prickly. "Hold up my chin, Slow-and-Solid. I'm going to try to learn to swim. It may be useful."

"Excellent!" said Slow-and-Solid; and he held up Stickly-Prickly's chin, while Stickly-Prickly kicked in the waters of the turbid Amazon.

"You'll make a fine swimmer yet," said Slow-and-Solid. "Now, if you can unlace my back-plates a little, I'll see what I can do towards curling up. It may be useful."

Stickly-Prickly helped to unlace Tortoise's back-plates, so that by twisting and straining Slow-and-Solid actually managed to curl up a tiddy wee bit.

"Excellent!" said Stickly-Prickly; "but I shouldn't do any more just now. It's making you black in the face. Kindly lead me into the water once again and I'll practise that side-stroke which you say is so easy." And so Stickly-Prickly practised, and Slow-and-Solid swam alongside.

"Excellent!" said Slow-and-Solid. "A little more prac-

18

tise will make you a regular whale. Now, if I may trouble you to unlace my back and front plates two holes more, I'll try that fascinating bend that you say is so easy. Won't Painted Jaguar be surprised!"

"Excellent!" said Stickly-Prickly, all wet from the turbid Amazon. "I declare, I shouldn't know you from one of my own family. Two holes, I think, you said? A little more expression, please, and don't grunt quite so much, or Painted Jaguar may hear us. When you've finished, I want to try that long dive which you say is so easy. Won't Painted Jaguar be surprised!"

And so Stickly-Prickly dived, and Slow-and-Solid dived alongside.

"Excellent!" said Slow-and-Solid. "A leetle more attention to holding your breath and you will be able to keep house at the bottom of the turbid Amazon. Now I'll try that exercise of wrapping my hind legs round my ears which you say is so peculiarly comfortable. Won't Painted Jaguar be surprised!"

"Excellent!" said Stickly-Prickly. "But it's straining your back-plates a little. They are all overlapping now, instead of lying side by side."

"Oh, that's the result of exercise," said Slow-and-Solid. "I've noticed that your prickles seem to be melting into one another, and that you're growing to look rather more like a pine-cone, and less like a chestnut-burr, than you used to."

"Am I?" said Stickly-Prickly. "That comes from my soaking in the water. Oh, won't Painted Jaguar be surprised!"

They went on with their exercises, each helping the other, till morning came; and when the sun was high they rested and dried themselves. Then they saw that they were both of them quite different from what they had been.

"Stickly-Prickly," said Tortoise after breakfast, "I am not what I was yesterday; but I think that I may yet amuse Painted Jaguar."

"That was the very thing I was thinking just now," said Stickly-Prickly. "I think scales are a tremendous improvement on prickles — to say nothing of being able to swim. Oh, *won't* Painted Jaguar be surprised! Let's go and find him."

By and by they found Painted Jaguar, still nursing his paddy-paw that had been hurt the night before. He was so astonished that he fell three times backward over his own painted tail without stopping.

They went on with their exercises, each helping the other.

"Good morning!" said Stickly-Prickly. "And how is your dear gracious Mummy this morning?"

"She is quite well, thank you," said Painted Jaguar; "but you must forgive me if I do not at this precise moment recall your name."

"That's unkind of you," said Stickly-Prickly, "seeing that this time yesterday you tried to scoop me out of my shell with your paw."

"But you hadn't any shell. It was all prickles," said Painted Jaguar. "I know it was. Just look at my paw!"

"You told me to drop into the turbid Amazon and be drowned," said Slow-and-Solid. "Why are you so rude and forgetful today?"

"Don't you remember what your mother told you?" said Stickly-Prickly, —

> *"Can't curl, but can swim —*
> *Stickly-Prickly, that's him!*
> *Curls up, but can't swim —*
> *Slow-Solid, that's him!"*

Then they both curled themselves up and rolled round and round Painted Jaguar till his eyes turned truly cartwheels in his head.

Then he went to fetch his mother.

"Mother," he said, "there are two new animals in the woods today, and the one that you said couldn't swim,

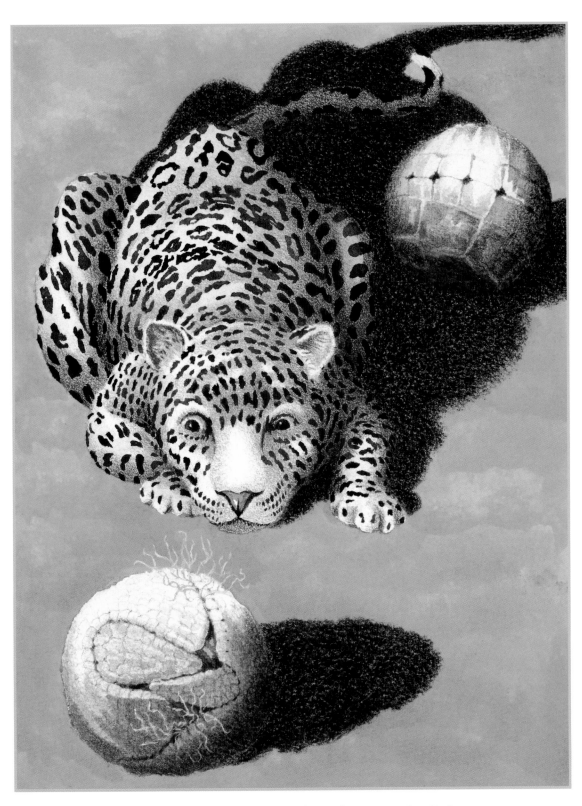

Then they both curled themselves up and rolled
round and round Painted Jaguar.

swims, and the one that you said couldn't curl up, curls; and they've gone shares in their prickles, I think, because both of them are scaly all over, instead of one being smooth and the other very prickly; and, besides that, they are rolling round and round in circles, and I don't feel comfy."

"Son, son!" said Mother Jaguar ever so many times, graciously waving her tail, "a Hedgehog is a Hedgehog, and can't be anything but a Hedgehog; and a Tortoise is a Tortoise, and can never be anything else."

"But it isn't a Hedgehog, and it isn't a Tortoise. It's a little bit of both, and I don't know its proper name."

"Nonsense!" said Mother Jaguar. "Everything has its proper name. I should call it 'Armadillo' till I found out the real one. And I should leave it alone."

So Painted Jaguar did as he was told, especially about leaving them alone; but the curious thing is that from that day to this, O Best Beloved, no one on the banks of the turbid Amazon has ever called Stickly-Prickly and Slow-and-Solid anything except Armadillo. There are Hedgehogs and Tortoises in other places, of course (there are some in my garden); but the real old and clever kind, with their scales lying lippety-lappety one over the other, like pine-cone scales, that lived on the banks of the turbid Amazon in the High and Far-Off Days, are always called Armadilloes, because they were so clever.

So *that's* all right, Best Beloved. Do you see?

I'VE NEVER *sailed the Amazon,*
    I've never reached Brazil;
But the Don *and* Magdalena,
    They can go there when they will!
        Yes, weekly from Southampton,
        Great steamers, white and gold,
        Go rolling down to Rio
        (Roll down — roll down to Rio!),
        And I'd like to roll to Rio
        Some day before I'm old!

I've never seen a Jaguar,
    Nor yet an Armadill —
O dilloing in his armour,
    And I s'pose I never will,
        Unless I go to Rio
        These wonders to behold —
        Roll down — roll down to Rio —
        Roll really down to Rio!
        Oh, I'd love to roll to Rio
        Some day before I'm old!

HOW THE FIRST LETTER
WAS WRITTEN

"Here's a pretty kettle of fish!" said Tegumai. "It will take me half the day to mend this!"

ONCE UPON A MOST early time was a Neolithic man. He was not a Jute or an Angle, or even a Dravidian, which he might well have been, Best Beloved, but never mind why. He was a Primitive, and he lived cavily in a Cave, and he wore very few clothes, and he couldn't read and he couldn't write and he didn't want to, and except when he was hungry he was quite happy. His name was Tegumai Bopsulai, and that means, "Man-who-does-not-put-his-foot-forward-in-a-hurry"; but we, O Best Beloved, will call him Tegumai, for short. And his wife's name was Teshumai Tewindrow, and that means, "Lady-who-asks-a-very-many-questions"; but we, O Best Beloved, will call her Teshumai, for short. And his little girl-daughter's name was Taffimai Metallumai, and that means, "Small-person-without-any-manners-who-ought-to-be-spanked"; but I'm going to call her Taffy. And she was Tegumai Bopsulai's Best Beloved and her own Mummy's Best Beloved, and she was not spanked half as much as was good for her; and they were all three very happy. As soon as Taffy could run about she went everywhere with her Daddy Tegumai, and sometimes they would not come home to the Cave till they were hungry, and then Teshumai Tewindrow would say, "Where in the world have you two been to, to get so shocking dirty? Really, my Tegumai, you're no better than my Taffy."

Now attend and listen!

One day Tegumai Bopsulai went down through the beaver-swamp to the Wagai river to spear carp-fish for dinner, and Taffy went too. Tegumai's spear was made of wood with shark's teeth at the end, and before he had caught any fish at all he accidentally broke it clean across by jabbing it down too hard on the bottom of the river. They were miles and miles from home (of course they had their lunch with them in a little bag), and Tegumai had forgotten to bring any extra spears.

"Here's a pretty kettle of fish!" said Tegumai. "It will take me half the day to mend this."

"There's your big black spear at home," said Taffy. "Let me run back to the Cave and ask Mummy to give it me."

"It's too far for your little fat legs," said Tegumai. "Besides, you might fall into the beaver-swamp and be drowned. We must make the best of a bad job." He sat down and took out a little leather mendy-bag, full of reindeer-sinews and strips of leather, and lumps of beeswax and resin, and began to mend the spear. Taffy sat down too, with her toes in the water and her chin in her hand, and thought very hard. Then she said: —

"I say, Daddy, it's an awful nuisance that you and I don't know how to write, isn't it? If we did we could send a message for the new spear."

"Taffy," said Tegumai, "how often have I told you not to use slang? 'Awful' isn't a pretty word, — but it *would* be a convenience, now you mention it, if we could write home."

Just then a Stranger-man came along the river, but he belonged to a far tribe, the Tewaras, and he did not understand one word of Tegumai's language. He stood on the bank and smiled at Taffy, because he had a little girl-daughter of his own at home. Tegumai drew a hank of deer-sinews from his mendy-bag and began to mend his spear.

"Come here," said Taffy. "Do you know where my Mummy lives?" And the Stranger-man said "Um!" — being, as you know, a Tewara.

"Silly!" said Taffy, and she stamped her foot, because she saw a shoal of very big carp going up the river just when her Daddy couldn't use his spear.

"Don't bother grown-ups," said Tegumai, so busy with his spear-mending that he did not turn round.

"I aren't," said Taffy. "I only want him to do what I want him to do, and he won't understand."

"Then don't bother me," said Tegumai, and he went on pulling and straining at the deer-sinews with his mouth full of loose ends. The Stranger-man — a genuine Tewara

"This is a very, very wonderful child."

he was — sat down on the grass, and Taffy showed him what her Daddy was doing. The Stranger-man thought, "This is a very wonderful child. She stamps her foot at me and she makes faces. She must be the daughter of that noble Chief who is so great that he won't take any notice of me." So he smiled more politely than ever.

"Now," said Taffy, "I want you to go to my Mummy, because your legs are longer than mine, and you won't fall into the beaver-swamp, and ask for Daddy's other spear — the one with the black handle that hangs over our fireplace."

The Stranger-man (*and* he was a Tewara) thought, "This is a very, very wonderful child. She waves her arms and she shouts at me, but I don't understand a word of what she says. But if I don't do what she wants, I greatly fear that that haughty Chief, Man-who-turns-his-back-on-callers, will be angry." He got up and twisted a big flat piece of bark off a birch-tree and gave it to Taffy. He did this, Best Beloved, to show that his heart was as white as the birch-bark and that he meant no harm; but Taffy didn't quite understand.

"Oh!" said she. "Now I see! You want my Mummy's living-address? Of course I can't write, but I can draw pictures if I've anything sharp to scratch with. Please lend me the shark's tooth off your necklace."

The Stranger-man (and *he* was a Tewara) didn't say anything, so Taffy put up her little hand and pulled at the beautiful bead and seed and shark-tooth necklace round his neck.

The Stranger-man (and he *was* a Tewara) thought, "This is a very, very wonderful child. The shark's tooth on my necklace is a magic shark's tooth, and I was always told that if anybody touched it without my leave they would immediately swell up or burst. But this child doesn't swell up or burst, and that important Chief, Man-who-attends-strictly-to-his-business, who has not yet taken any notice of me at all, doesn't seem to be afraid that she will swell up or burst. I had better be more polite."

So he gave Taffy the shark's tooth, and she lay down flat on her tummy with her legs in the air, like some people on the drawing-room floor when they want to draw pictures, and she said, "Now I'll draw you some beautiful pictures! You can look over my shoulder, but you mustn't joggle. First I'll draw Daddy fishing. It isn't very like him; but Mummy will know, because I've drawn his spear all broken. Well, now I'll draw the other spear that he wants, the black-handled spear. It looks as if it was sticking in Daddy's back, but that's because the shark's tooth slipped and this piece of bark isn't big enough. That's the spear I want you to fetch; so I'll draw a picture of me myself 'splaining to you. My hair doesn't stand up like I've drawn, but it's easier to draw that way. Now I'll draw you. *I* think you're very nice really, but I can't make you pretty in the picture, so you mustn't be 'fended. Are you 'fended?"

The Stranger-man (and he was *a* Tewara) smiled. He thought, "There must be a big battle going to be fought somewhere, and this extraordinary child, who takes my magic shark's tooth but who does not swell up or burst, is telling me to call all the great Chief's tribe to help him. He *is* a great Chief, or he would have noticed me."

"Look," said Taffy, drawing very hard and rather scratchily, "now I've drawn you, and I've put the spear that Daddy wants into your hand, just to remind you that you're to bring it. Now I'll show you how to find my Mummy's living-address. You go along till you come to two trees (those are trees), and then you go over a hill (that's a hill), and then you come into a beaver-swamp all full of beavers. I haven't put in all the beavers, because I can't draw beavers, but I've drawn their heads, and that's all you'll see of them when you cross the swamp. Mind you don't fall in! Then our Cave is just beyond the beaver-swamp. It isn't as high as the hills really, but I can't draw things very small. That's my Mummy outside. She is beautiful. She is the most beautifullest Mummy there ever was, but she won't be 'fended when she sees I've drawn her so plain. She'll be pleased of me because I can draw. Now, in case you forget, I've drawn the spear that Daddy wants *outside* our Cave. It's *inside* really, but you show the picture to my Mummy and she'll give it you. I've made her holding up her hands, because I know she'll be so pleased to see you. Isn't it a beautiful picture? And do you quite understand, or shall I 'splain again?"

The Stranger-man (and he was a *Tewara*) looked at the picture and nodded very hard. He said to himself, "If I do not fetch this great Chief's tribe to help him, he will be slain by his enemies who are coming up on all sides with spears. Now I see why the great Chief pretended not to notice me! He feared that his enemies were hiding in the bushes and would see him deliver a message to me.

Therefore he turned his back, and let the wise and wonderful child draw the terrible picture showing me his difficulties. I will away and get help for him from his tribe." He did not even ask Taffy the road, but raced off into the bushes like the wind, with the birch-bark in his hand, and Taffy sat down most pleased.

Now this is the picture that Taffy had drawn for him!

"What have you been doing, Taffy?" said Tegumai. He

Now this is the picture that Taffy had drawn for him!

37

had mended his spear and was carefully waving it to and fro.

"It's a little berangement of my own, Daddy dear," said Taffy. "If you won't ask me questions, you'll know all about it in a little time, and you'll be surprised. You don't know how surprised you'll be, Daddy! Promise you'll be surprised."

"Very well," said Tegumai, and went on fishing.

The Stranger-man — did you know he was a Tewara? — hurried away with the picture and ran for some miles, till quite by accident he found Teshumai Tewindrow at the door of her Cave, talking to some other Neolithic ladies who had come in to a Primitive lunch. Taffy was very like Teshumai, specially about the upper part of the face and the eyes, so the Stranger-man — always a pure Tewara — smiled politely and handed Teshumai the birch-bark. He had run hard, so that he panted, and his legs were scratched with brambles, but he still tried to be polite.

As soon as Teshumai saw the picture she screamed like anything and flew at the Stranger-man. The other Neolithic ladies at once knocked him down and sat on him in a long line of six, while Teshumai pulled his hair. "It's as plain as the nose on this Stranger-man's face," she said. "He has stuck my Tegumai all full of spears, and frightened poor Taffy so that her hair stands all on end; and not content with that, he brings me a horrid picture of how it was done. Look!" She showed the picture to all the Neolithic

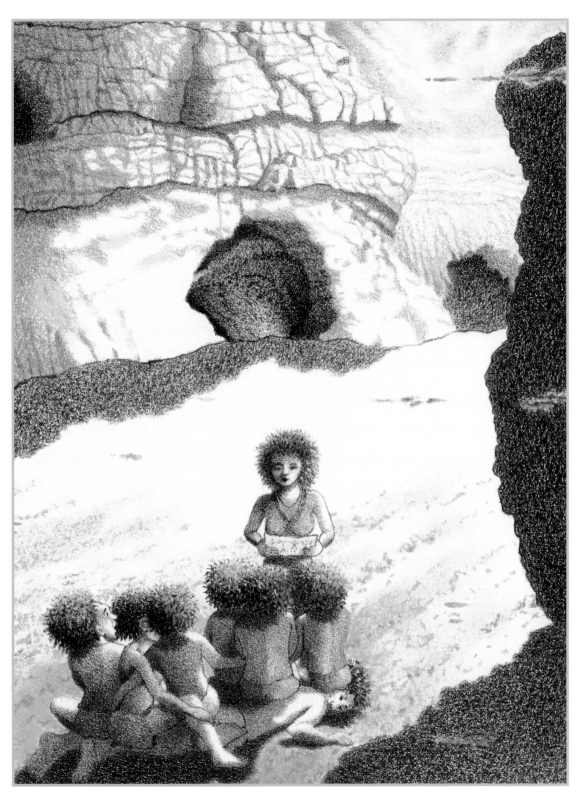

*The other Neolithic ladies at once knocked him down
and sat on him.*

ladies sitting patiently on the Stranger-man. "Here is my Tegumai with his arm broken; here is a spear sticking into his back; here is a man with a spear ready to throw; here is another man throwing a spear from a Cave, and here are a whole pack of people" (they were Taffy's beavers really, but they did look rather like people) "coming up behind Tegumai. Isn't it shocking!"

"Most shocking!" said the Neolithic ladies, and they filled the Stranger-man's hair with mud (at which he was surprised), and they beat upon the Reverberating Tribal Drums, and called together all the Chiefs of the Tribe of Tegumai, with their Hetmans and Dolmans, all Neguses, Woons, and Akhoonds of the organisation, in addition to the Warlocks, Angekoks, Juju-men, Bonzes, and the rest, who decided that before they chopped the Stranger-man's head off he should instantly lead them down to the river and show them where he had hidden poor Taffy.

By this time the Stranger-man (in spite of being a Tewara) was really annoyed. They had filled his hair quite solid with mud; they had rolled him up and down on knobby pebbles; they had sat upon him in a long line of six; they had thumped him and bumped him till he could hardly breathe; and though he did not understand their language, he was almost sure that the names the Neolithic ladies called him were not ladylike. However, he said nothing till all the Tribe of Tegumai were assembled, and then he led them back to the bank of the Wagai river, and there they found Taffy making daisy-chains, and Tegumai carefully spearing small carp with his mended spear.

"Well, you *have* been quick!" said Taffy. "But why did you bring so many people? Daddy, dear, this is my surprise. *Are* you surprised, Daddy?"

"Very," said Tegumai; "but it has ruined all my fishing for the day. Why, the whole dear, kind, nice, clean, quiet Tribe is here, Taffy."

And so they were. First of all walked Teshumai Tewindrow and the Neolithic ladies, tightly holding on to the Stranger-man, whose hair was full of mud (although he was a Tewara). Behind them came the Head Chief, the Vice-Chief, the Deputy and Assistant Chiefs (all armed to the upper teeth), the Hetmans and Heads of Hundreds, Platoffs with their Platoons, and Dolmans with their Detachments; Woons, Neguses, and Akhoonds ranking in the rear (still armed to the teeth). Behind them was the Tribe in hierarchical order, from owners of four caves (one for each season), a private reindeer-run, and two salmon-leaps, to feudal and prognathous Villeins, semi-entitled to half a bearskin of winter nights, seven yards from the fire, and adscript serfs, holding the reversion of a scraped marrow-bone under heriot (Aren't those beautiful words, Best Beloved?). They were all there, prancing and shouting, and they frightened every fish for twenty miles, and Tegumai thanked them in a fluid Neolithic oration.

Then Teshumai Tewindrow ran down and kissed and

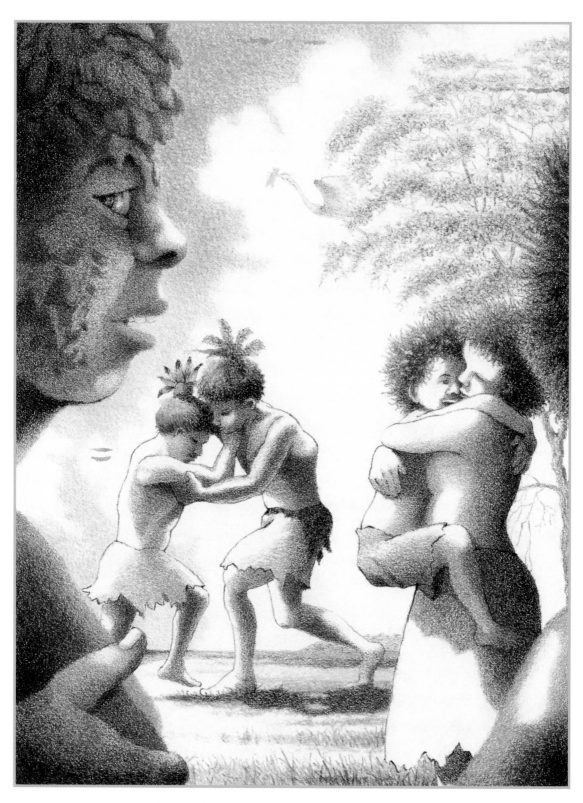

Then Teshumai Tewindrow ran down and kissed
and hugged Taffy very much indeed.

hugged Taffy very much indeed; but the Head Chief of the Tribe of Tegumai took Tegumai by the top-knot feathers and shook him severely.

"Explain! Explain! Explain!" cried all the Tribe of Tegumai.

"Goodness' sakes alive!" said Tegumai. "Let go of my top-knot. Can't a man break his carp-spear without the whole countryside descending on him? You're a very interfering people."

"I don't believe you've brought my Daddy's black-handled spear after all," said Taffy. "And what *are* you doing to my nice Stranger-man?"

They were thumping him by twos and threes and tens till his eyes turned round and round. He could only gasp and point at Taffy.

"Where are the bad people who speared you, my darling?" said Teshumai Tewindrow.

"There weren't any," said Tegumai. "My only visitor this morning was the poor fellow that you are trying to choke. Aren't you well, or are you ill, O Tribe of Tegumai?"

"He came with a horrible picture," said the Head Chief, — "a picture that showed you were full of spears."

"Er — um — P'raps I'd better 'splain that I gave him that picture," said Taffy, but she did not feel quite comfy.

"You!" said the Tribe of Tegumai all together. "Small-person-with-no-manners-who-ought-to-be-spanked! You?"

"Taffy dear, I'm afraid we're in for a little trouble," said her Daddy, and put his arm round her, so she didn't care.

"Explain! Explain! Explain!" said the Head Chief of the Tribe of Tegumai, and he hopped on one foot.

"I wanted the Stranger-man to fetch Daddy's spear, so I drawded it," said Taffy. "There wasn't lots of spears. There was only one spear. I drawded it three times to make sure. I couldn't help it looking as if it stuck into Daddy's head — there wasn't room on the birch-bark; and those things that Mummy called bad people are my beavers. I drawded them to show him the way through the swamp; and I drawded Mummy at the mouth of the Cave looking pleased because he is a nice Stranger-man, and *I* think you are just the stupidest people in the world," said Taffy. "He is a very nice man. Why have you filled his hair with mud? Wash him!"

Nobody said anything at all for a long time, till the Head Chief laughed; then the Stranger-man (who was at least a Tewara) laughed; then Tegumai laughed till he fell down flat on the bank; then all the Tribe laughed more and worse and louder. The only people who did not laugh were Teshumai Tewindrow and all the Neolithic ladies. They were very polite to all their husbands, and said "Idiot!" ever so often.

Then the Head Chief of the Tribe of Tegumai cried and said and sang, "O Small-person-without-any-manners-who-ought-to-be-spanked, you've hit upon a great invention!"

"I didn't intend to; I only wanted Daddy's black-handled spear," said Taffy.

"Never mind. It *is* a great invention, and some day men will call it writing. At present it is only pictures, and, as we have seen today, pictures are not always properly understood. But a time will come, O Babe of Tegumai, when we shall make letters — all twenty-six of 'em, — and when we shall be able to read as well as to write, and then we shall always say exactly what we mean without any mistakes. Let the Neolithic ladies wash the mud out of the stranger's hair!"

"I shall be glad of that," said Taffy, "because, after all, though you've brought every single other spear in the Tribe of Tegumai, you've forgotten my Daddy's black-handled spear."

Then the Head Chief cried and said and sang, "Taffy, dear, the next time you write a picture-letter, you'd better send a man who can talk our language with it, to explain what it means. I don't mind it myself, because I am a Head Chief, but it's very bad for the rest of the Tribe of Tegumai, and, as you can see, it surprises the stranger."

Then they adopted the Stranger-man (a genuine Tewara of Tewar) into the Tribe of Tegumai, because he was a gentleman and did not make a fuss about the mud that the Neolithic ladies had put into his hair. But from that day to this (and I suppose it is all Taffy's fault), very few little girls have ever liked learning to read or write.

Most of them prefer to draw pictures and play about with their Daddies — just like Taffy.

THERE RUNS *a road by Merrow Down —*
  A grassy track today it is —
An hour out of Guildford town,
  Above the river Wey it is.

Here, when they heard the horse-bells ring,
  The ancient Britons dressed and rode
To watch the dark Phoenicians bring
  Their goods along the Western Road.

And here, or hereabouts, they met
  To hold their racial talks and such —
To barter beads for Whitby jet,
  And tin for gay shell torques and such.

But long and long before that time
  (When bison used to roam on it)
Did Taffy and her Daddy climb
  That down, and had their home on it.

Then beavers built in Broadstonebrook
  And made a swamp where Bramley stands;
And bears from Shere would come and look
  For Taffimai where Shamley stands.

46

The Wey, that Taffy called Wagai,
  Was more than six times bigger then;
And all the Tribe of Tegumai
  They cut a noble figure then!

HOW THE ALPHABET
WAS MADE

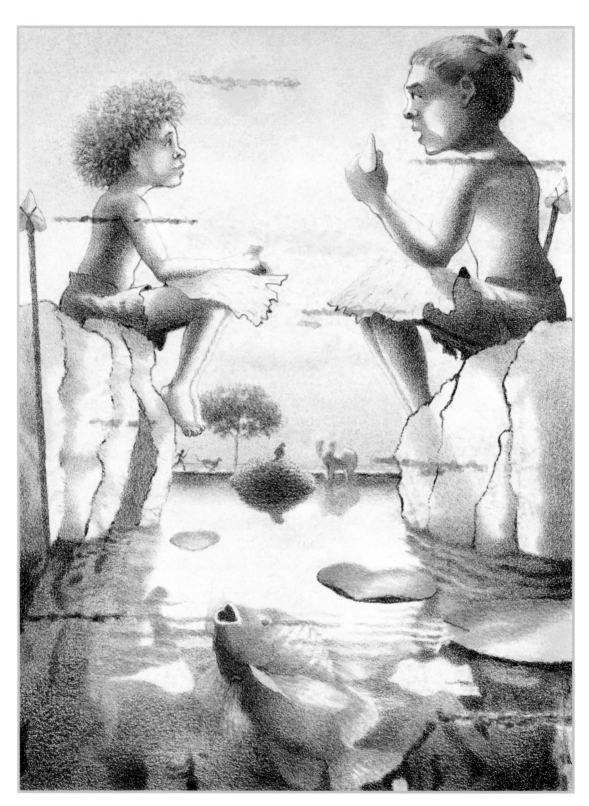

"Ah! ah! ah!" said her Daddy.

THE WEEK after Taffimai Metallumai (we will still call her Taffy, Best Beloved) made that little mistake about her Daddy's spear and the Stranger-man and the picture-letter and all, she went carp-fishing again with her Daddy. Her Mummy wanted her to stay at home and help hang up hides to dry on the big drying-poles outside their Neolithic Cave, but Taffy slipped away down to her Daddy quite early, and they fished. Presently she began to giggle, and her Daddy said, "Don't be silly, child."

"But wasn't it inciting!" said Taffy. "Don't you remember how the Head Chief puffed out his cheeks, and how funny the nice Stranger-man looked with the mud in his hair?"

"Well do I," said Tegumai. "I had to pay two deerskins — soft ones with fringes — to the Stranger-man for the things we did to him."

"*We* didn't do anything," said Taffy. "It was Mummy and the other Neolithic ladies — and the mud."

"We won't talk about that," said her Daddy. "Let's have lunch."

Taffy took a marrow-bone and sat mousy-quiet for ten whole minutes, while her Daddy scratched on pieces of birch-bark with a shark's tooth. Then she said, "Daddy, I've thinked of a secret surprise. You make a noise — any sort of noise."

"Ah!" said Tegumai. "Will that do to begin with?"

"Yes," said Taffy. "You look just like a carp-fish with its mouth open. Say it again, please."

"Ah! ah! ah!" said her Daddy. "Don't be rude, my daughter."

"I'm not meaning rude, really and truly," said Taffy. "It's part of my secret-surprise-think. *Do* say *ah*, Daddy, and keep your mouth open at the end, and lend me that tooth. I'm going to draw a carp-fish's mouth wide-open."

"What for?" said her Daddy.

"Don't you see?" said Taffy, scratching away on the bark. "That will be our little secret s'prise. When I draw a carp-fish with his mouth open in the smoke at the back of our Cave — if Mummy doesn't mind — it will remind you of that ah-noise. Then we can play that it was me jumped out of the dark and s'prised you with that noise — same as I did in the beaver-swamp last winter."

"Really?" said her Daddy, in the voice that grown-ups use when they are truly attending. "Go on, Taffy."

"Oh bother!" she said. "I can't draw all of a carp-fish, but I can draw something that means a carp-fish's mouth. Don't you know how they stand on their heads rooting in the mud? Well, here's a pretence carp-fish (we can play that the rest of him is drawn). Here's just his mouth, and that means *ah.*" And she drew this. (1.)

1

"That's not bad," said Tegumai, and scratched on his own piece of bark for himself; "but you've forgotten the feeler that hangs across his mouth."

"But I can't draw, Daddy."

"You needn't draw anything of him except just the opening of his mouth and the feeler across. Then we'll know he's a carp-fish, 'cause the perches and trouts haven't got feelers. Look here, Taffy." And he drew this. (2.)

2

"Now I'll copy it." said Taffy. "Will you understand *this* when you see it?"

And she drew this. (3.)

3

"Perfectly," said her Daddy. "And I'll be quite as s'prised when I see it anywhere, as if you had jumped out from behind a tree and said 'Ah!'"

"Now, make another noise," said Taffy, very proud.

"Yah!" said her Daddy, very loud.

"H'm," said Taffy. "That's a mixy noise. The end part is *ah*-carp-fish-mouth; but what can we do about the front part? *Yer-yer-yer* and *ah! Yah!*"

"It's very like the carp-fish-mouth noise. Let's draw another bit of the carp-fish and join 'em," said her Daddy. *He* was quite incited too.

53

"No. If they're joined, I'll forget. Draw it separate. Draw his tail. If he's standing on his head the tail will come first. 'Sides, I think I can draw tails easiest," said Taffy.

"A good notion," said Tegumai. "Here's a carp-fish tail for the *yer*-noise." And he drew this. (4.)

4

"I'll try now," said Taffy. "'Member I can't draw like you, Daddy. Will it do if I just draw the split part of the tail, and a sticky-down line for where it joins?" And she drew this. (5.)

5

Her Daddy nodded, and his eyes were shiny bright with 'citement.

"That's beautiful," she said. "Now make another noise, Daddy."

"Oh!" said her Daddy, very loud.

"That's quite easy," said Taffy. "You make your mouth all round like an egg or a stone. So an egg or a stone will do for that."

"You can't always find eggs or stones. We'll have to scratch a round something like one." And he drew this. (6.)

6

"My gracious!" said Taffy, "what a lot of noise-pictures we've made, — carp-mouth, carp-tail, and egg! Now, make another noise, Daddy."

"Ssh!" said her Daddy, and frowned to himself, but Taffy was too incited to notice.

"That's quite easy," she said, scratching on the bark.

"Eh, what?" said her Daddy. "I meant I was thinking, and didn't want to be disturbed."

"It's a noise, just the same. It's the noise a snake makes, Daddy, when it is thinking and doesn't want to be disturbed. Let's make the *ssh*-noise a snake. Will this do?" And she drew this. (7.)

7

"There," she said. "That's another s'prise-secret. When you draw a hissy-snake by the door of your little back-cave where you mend the spears, I'll know you're thinking hard; and I'll come in most mousy-quiet. And if you draw it on a tree by the river when you're fishing, I'll know you want me to walk most *most* mousy-quiet, so as not to shake the banks."

"Perfectly true," said Tegumai. "And there's more in this game than you think. Taffy, dear, I've a notion that your Daddy's daughter has hit upon the finest thing that there ever was since the Tribe of Tegumai took to using shark's teeth instead of flints for their spear-heads. I believe we've found out *the* big secret of the world."

"Why?" said Taffy, and her eyes shone too with incitement.

"I'll show," said her Daddy. "What's water in the Tegumai language?"

"*Ya*, of course, and it means river too — like Wagai-*ya* — the Wagai river."

"What is bad water that gives you fever if you drink it — black water — swamp-water?"

55

"*Yo*, of course."

"Now look," said her Daddy. "S'pose you saw this scratched by the side of a pool in the beaver-swamp?" And he drew this. (8.)

8

"Carp-tail and round egg. Two noises mixed! Yo, bad water," said Taffy. "'Course I wouldn't drink that water because I'd know you said it was bad."

"But I needn't be near the water at all. I might be miles away, hunting, and still —"

"And *still* it would be just the same as if you stood there and said, 'G'way, Taffy, or you'll get fever.' All that in a carp-fish-tail and a round egg! Oh, Daddy, we must tell Mummy, quick!" and Taffy danced all round him.

"Not yet," said Tegumai; "not till we've gone a little further. Let's see. *Yo* is bad water, but *so* is food cooked on the fire, isn't it?" And he drew this. (9.)

9

"Yes. Snake and egg," said Taffy. "So that means dinner's ready. If you saw that scratched on a tree you'd know it was time to come to the Cave. So'd I."

"My Winkie!" said Tegumai. "That's true too. But wait a minute. I see a difficulty. *So* means 'come and have dinner,' but *sho* means the drying-poles where we hang our hides."

"Horrid old drying-poles!" said Taffy. "I hate helping to hang heavy, hot, hairy hides on them. If you drew the snake and egg, and I thought it meant dinner, and I came in from the wood and found that it meant I was to help Mummy hang the hides on the drying-poles, what *would* I do?"

"You'd be cross. So'd Mummy. We must make a new picture for *sho*. We must draw a spotty snake that hisses *sh-sh*, and we'll play that the plain snake only hisses *ssss*."

"I couldn't be sure how to put in the spots," said Taffy. "And p'raps if *you* were in a hurry you might leave them out, and I'd think it was *so* when it was *sho*, and then Mummy would catch me just the same. *No!* I think we'd better draw a picture of the horrid high drying-poles their very selves, and make *quite* sure. I'll put 'em in just after the hissy-snake. Look!" And she drew this. (10.)

"P'raps that's safest. It's very like our drying-poles, any-how," said her Daddy, laughing. "Now I'll make a new noise with a snake and drying-pole sound in it. I'll say *shi*. That's Tegumai for spear, Taffy." And he laughed.

"Don't make fun of me," said Taffy, as she thought of her picture-letter and the mud in the Stranger-man's hair. "*You* draw it, Daddy."

"We won't have beavers or hills this time, eh?" said her Daddy. "I'll just draw a straight line for my spear." And he drew this. (11.)

"Even Mummy couldn't mistake that for me being killed."

"*Please* don't, Daddy. It makes me uncomfy. Do some more noises. We're getting on beautifully."

"Er-hm!" said Tegumai, looking up. "We'll say *shu*. That means sky."

Taffy drew the snake and the drying-pole. Then she stopped. "We must make a new picture for that end sound, mustn't we?"

"*Shu-shu-u-u-u!*" said her Daddy. "Why, it's just like the round-egg-sound made thin."

"Then s'pose we draw a thin round egg, and pretend it's a frog that hasn't eaten anything for years."

"N-no," said her Daddy. "If we drew that in a hurry we might mistake it for the round egg itself. *Shu-shu-shu! I'll* tell you what we'll do. We'll open a little hole at the end of the round egg to show how the O-noise runs out all thin, *ooo-oo-oo*. Like this." And he drew this. (12.)

12

"Oh, that's lovely! Much better than a thin frog. Go on," said Taffy, using her shark's tooth.

Her Daddy went on drawing, and his hand shook with incitement. He went on till he had drawn this. (13.)

13

"Don't look up, Taffy," he said. "Try if you can make

58

out what that means in the Tegumai language. If you can, we've found the Secret."

"Snake — pole — broken-egg — carp-tail and carp-mouth," said Taffy. "*Shu-ya*. Sky-water [rain]." Just then a drop fell on her hand, for the day had clouded over. "Why, Daddy, it's raining. Was *that* what you meant to tell me?"

"Of course," said her Daddy. "And I told it you without saying a word, didn't I?"

"Well, I *think* I would have known it in a minute, but that raindrop made me quite sure. I'll always remember now. *Shu-ya* means rain, or 'it is going to rain.' Why, Daddy!" She got up and danced round him. "S'pose you went out before I was awake, and drawed *shu-ya* in the smoke on the wall, I'd know it was going to rain and I'd take my beaver-skin hood. Wouldn't Mummy be s'rprised!"

Tegumai got up and danced. (Daddies didn't mind doing those things in those days.) "More than that! More than that!" he said. "S'pose I wanted to tell you it wasn't going to rain much and you must come down to the river, what would we draw? Say the words in Tegumai-talk first."

"*Shu-ya-las, ya maru.* [Sky-water ending. River come to.] *What* a lot of new sounds! *I* don't see how we can draw them."

"But I do — but I do!" said Tegumai. "Just attend a minute, Taffy, and we won't do any more today. We've got *shu-ya* all right, haven't we? but this *las* is a teaser. *La-la-la!*" and he waved his shark-tooth.

"There's the hissy-snake at the end and the carp-mouth before the snake — *as-as-as*. We only want *la-la*," said Taffy.

"I know it, but we have to make *la-la*. And we're the first people in all the world who've ever tried to do it, Taffi-mai!"

"Well," said Taffy, yawning, for she was rather tired. "*Las* means breaking or finishing as well as ending, doesn't it?"

"So it does," said Tegumai. "*Ya-las* means that there's no water in the tank for Mummy to cook with — just when I'm going hunting, too."

"And *shi-las* means that your spear is broken. If I'd only thought of *that* instead of drawing silly beaver-pictures for the Stranger-man!"

"*La! La! La!*" said Tegumai, waving his stick and frowning. "Oh, bother!"

"I could have drawn *shi* quite easily," Taffy went on. "Then I'd have drawn your spear all broken — this way!" And she drew. (14.)

14

"The very thing," said Tegumai. "That's *la* all over. It isn't like any of the other marks, either." And he drew this. (15.)

15

"Now for *ya*. Oh, we've done that before. Now for *maru*. *Mum-mum-mum*. *Mum* shuts one's mouth up, doesn't it? We'll draw a shut mouth like this." And he drew. (16.)

16

60

"Then the carp-mouth open. That makes *Ma-ma-ma!* But what about this *rrrrr*-thing, Taffy?"

"It sounds all rough and edgy, like your shark-tooth saw when you're cutting out a plank for the canoe," said Taffy.

"You mean all sharp at the edges, like this?" said Tegumai. And he drew. (17.)

17

"'Xactly," said Taffy. "But we don't want all those teeth: only put two."

"I'll only put in one," said Tegumai. "If this game of ours is going to be what I think it will, the easier we make our sound-pictures the better for everybody." And he drew. (18.)

"*Now*, we've got it," said Tegumai, standing on one leg. "I'll draw 'em all in a string like fish."

18

"Hadn't we better put a little bit of stick or something between each word, so's they won't rub up against each other and jostle, same as if they were carps?"

"Oh, I'll leave a space for that," said her Daddy. And very incitedly he drew them all without stopping, on a big new bit of birch-bark. (19.)

19

"*Shu-ya-las ya-maru,*" said Taffy, reading it out sound by sound.

61

"That's enough for today," said Tegumai. "Besides, you're getting tired, Taffy. Never mind, dear. We'll finish it all tomorrow, and then we'll be remembered for years and years after the biggest trees you can see are all chopped up for firewood."

So they went home, and all that evening Tegumai sat on one side of the fire and Taffy on the other, drawing *ya*'s and *yo*'s and *shu*'s and *shi*'s in the smoke on the wall and giggling together till her Mummy said, "Really, Tegumai, you're worse than my Taffy."

"Please don't mind," said Taffy. "It's only our secret-s'prise, Mummy, dear, and we'll tell you all about it the very minute it's done; but *please* don't ask me what it is now, or else I'll have to tell."

So her Mummy most carefully didn't; and bright and early next morning Tegumai went down to the river to think about new sound-pictures, and when Taffy got up she saw *Ya-las* [water is ending or running out] chalked on the side of the big stone water-tank, outside the Cave.

"Um," said Taffy. "These picture-sounds are rather a bother! Daddy's just as good as come here himself and told me to get more water for Mummy to cook with." She went to the spring at the back of the Cave and filled the tank from a bark bucket, and then she ran down to the river and pulled her Daddy's left ear — the one that belonged to her to pull when she was good.

"Now come along and we'll draw all the left-over

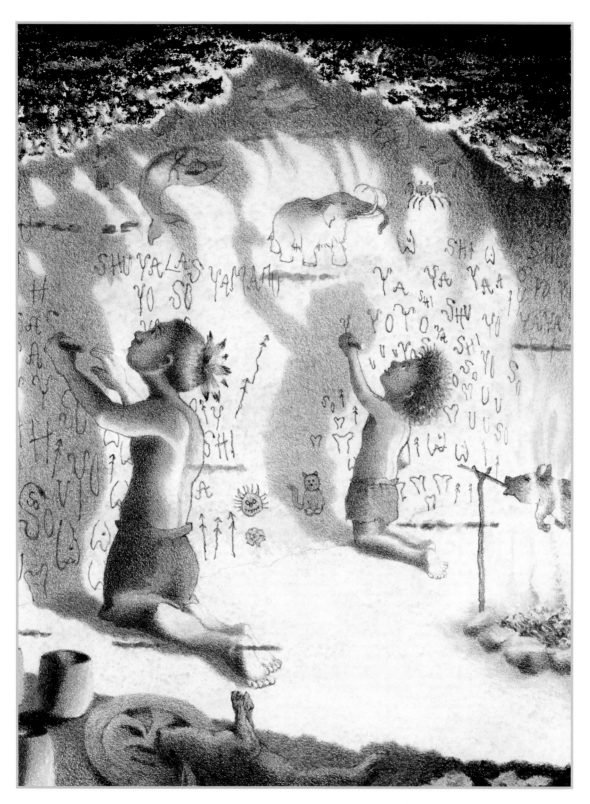

"It's only our secret-s'prise, Mummy, dear."

sound-pictures," said her Daddy, and they had a most inciting day of it, and a beautiful lunch in the middle, and
two games of romps. When they came to T, Taffy said that
as her name, and her Daddy's, and her Mummy's all began
with that sound, they should draw a sort of family group of
themselves holding hands. That was all very well to draw
once or twice; but when it came to drawing it six or seven
times, Taffy and Tegumai drew it scratchier and scratchier,
till at last the T-sound was only a thin long Tegumai with
his arms out to hold Taffy and Teshumai. You can see from
these three pictures partly how it happened. (20, 21, 22.)

Many of the other pictures were much too beautiful to

20, 21, 22, 23

begin with, especially before lunch; but as they were drawn
over and over again on birch-bark, they became plainer
and easier, till at last even Tegumai said he could find no
fault with them. They turned the hissy-snake the other way
round for the Z-sound, to show it was hissing backwards in
a soft and gentle way (23); and they just made a twiddle for
E, because it came into the pictures so often (24); and they
drew pictures of the sacred Beaver of the Tegumais for the

24, 25, 26, 27

B-sound (25, 26, 27, 28); and because it was a nasty, nosy noise, they just drew noses for the N-sound, till they were tired (29); and they drew a picture of the big lake-pike's mouth for the greedy Ga-sound (30); and they drew the pike's mouth again with a spear behind it for the scratchy,

28, 29, 30

hurty Ka-sound (31); and they drew pictures of a little bit of the winding Wagai river for the nice windy-windy Wa-sound (32, 33); and so on and so forth and so following till they had done and drawn all the sound-pictures that they wanted, and there was the Alphabet, all complete.

31, 32, 33

And after thousands and thousands and thousands of years, and after Hieroglyphics and Demotics, and Nilotics, and Cryptics, and Cufics, and Runics, and Dorics, and Ionics, and all sorts of other ricks and tricks (because the Woons, and the Neguses, and the Akhoonds, and the Repositories of Tradition would never leave a good thing alone when they saw it), the fine old easy, understandable

65

Alphabet — A, B, C, D, E, and the rest of 'em — got back into its proper shape again for all Best Beloveds to learn when they are old enough.

But *I* remember Tegumai Bopsulai, and Taffimai Metallumai, and Teshumai Tewindrow, her dear Mummy, and all the days gone by. And it was so — just so — a long time ago — on the banks of the big Wagai!

> OF ALL *the Tribe of Tegumai*
> *Who cut that figure, none remain,* —
> *On Merrow Down the cuckoos cry* —
> *The silence and the sun remain.*
>
> *But as the faithful years return*
> *And hearts unwounded sing again,*
> *Comes Taffy dancing through the fern*
> *To lead the Surrey spring again.*
>
> *Her brows are bound with bracken-fronds,*
> *And golden elf-locks fly above;*
> *Her eyes are bright as diamonds*
> *And bluer than the sky above.*
>
> *In moccasins and deer-skin cloak,*
> *Unfearing, free and fair she flits,*
> *And lights her little damp-wood smoke*
> *To show her Daddy where she flits.*

For far — oh, very far behind,
 So far she cannot call to him,
Comes Tegumai alone to find
 The daughter that was all to him.

THE CRAB THAT PLAYED WITH THE SEA

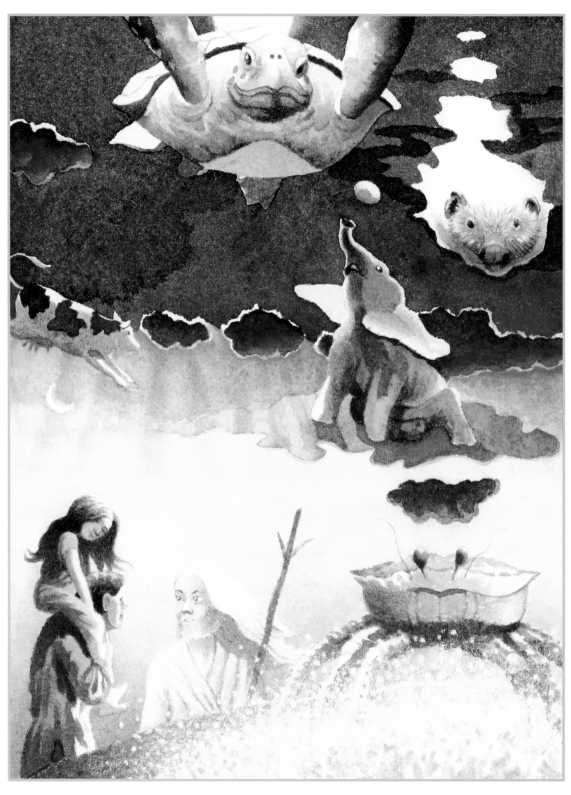

"Ho, Son of Adam, this is the play of the Very Beginning;
but you are too wise for this play."

BEFORE THE HIGH and Far-Off Times, O my Best Beloved, came the Time of the Very Beginnings; and that was in the days when the Eldest Magician was getting Things ready. First he got the Earth ready; then he got the Sea ready; and then he told all the Animals that they could come out and play. And the Animals said, "O Eldest Magician, what shall we play at?" and he said, "I will show you." He took the Elephant — All-the-Elephant-there-was — and said, "Play at being an Elephant," and All-the-Elephant-there-was played. He took the Beaver — All-the-Beaver-there-was — and said, "Play at being a Beaver," and All-the-Beaver-there-was played. He took the Cow — All-the Cow-there-was — and said, "Play at being a Cow," and All-the-Cow-there-was played. He took the Turtle — All-the-Turtle-there-was and said, "Play at being a Turtle," and All-the-Turtle-there-was played. One by one he took all the beasts and birds and fishes and told them what to play at.

But towards evening, when people and things grow restless and tired, there came up the Man (With his own little girl-daughter?) — Yes, with his own best-beloved little girl-daughter sitting upon his shoulder, and he said, "What is this play, Eldest Magician?" And the Eldest Magician said, "Ho, Son of Adam, this is the play of the Very Beginning; but you are too wise for this play." And the Man saluted and said, "Yes, I am too wise for this play; but see that you make all the Animals obedient to me."

Now, while the two were talking together, Pau Amma the Crab, who was next in the game, scuttled off sideways and stepped into the sea, saying to himself, "I will play my play alone in the deep waters, and I will never be obedient to this son of Adam." Nobody saw him go away except the little girl-daughter where she leaned on the Man's shoulder. And the play went on till there were no more Animals left without orders; and the Eldest Magician wiped the fine dust off his hands and walked about the world to see how the Animals were playing.

He went North, Best Beloved, and he found All-the-Elephant-there-was digging with his tusks and stamping with his feet in the nice new clean earth that had been made ready for him.

"*Kun?*" said All-the-Elephant-there-was, meaning, "Is this right?"

"*Payah kun,*" said the Eldest Magician, meaning, "That is quite right"; and he breathed upon the great rocks and lumps of earth that All-the-Elephant-there-was had thrown up, and they became the great Himalayan Mountains, and you can look them out on the map.

He went East, and he found All-the-Cow-there-was feeding in the field that had been made ready for her, and she licked her tongue round a whole forest at a time, and swallowed it and sat down to chew her cud.

"*Kun?*" said All-the-Cow-there-was.

"*Payah kun,*" said the Eldest Magician; and he breathed upon the bare patch where she had eaten, and upon the place where she had sat down, and one became the great Indian Desert, and the other became the Desert of Sahara, and you can look them out on the map.

He went West, and he found All-the-Beaver-there-was making a beaver-dam across the mouths of broad rivers that had been got ready for him.

"*Kun?*" said All-the-Beaver-there-was.

"*Payah kun,*" said the Eldest Magician; and he breathed upon the fallen trees and the still water, and they became the Everglades in Florida, and you may look them out on the map.

Then he went South and found All-the-Turtle-there-was scratching with his flippers in the sand that had been got ready for him, and the sand and the rocks whirled through the air and fell far off into the sea.

"*Kun?*" said All-the-Turtle-there-was.

"*Payah kun,*" said the Eldest Magician; and he breathed upon the sand and the rocks, where they had fallen in the sea, and they became the most beautiful islands of Borneo, Celebes, Sumatra, Java, and the rest of the Malay

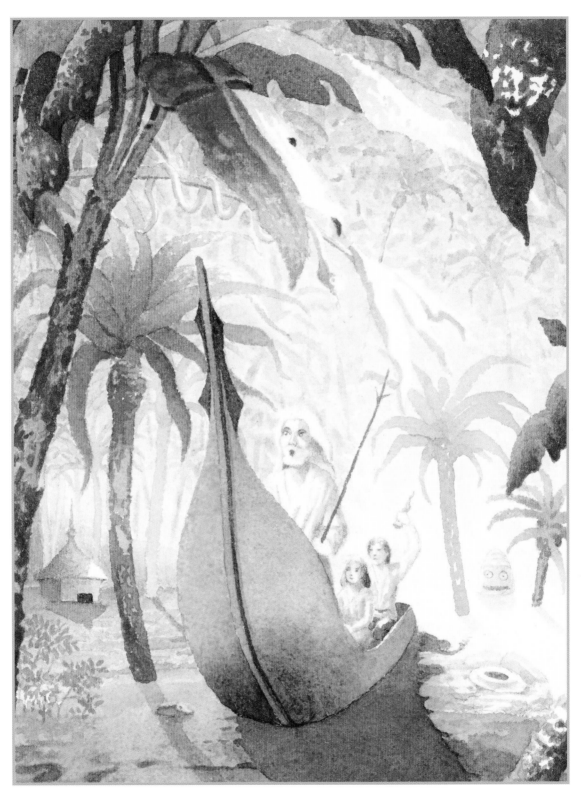

"Then the Sea began to run back and back, and the canoe was
sucked out of the mouth of the Perak River."

Archipelago, and you can look *them* out on the map!

By and by the Eldest Magician met the Man on the banks of the Perak River, and said, "Ho! Son of Adam, are all the Animals obedient to you?"

"Yes," said the Man.

"Is all the Earth obedient to you?"

"Yes," said the Man.

"Is all the Sea obedient to you?"

"No," said the Man. "Once a day and once a night the Sea runs up the Perak River and drives the sweet water back into the forest, so that my house is made wet; once a day and once a night it runs down the river and draws all the water after it, so that there is nothing left but mud, and my canoe is upset. Is that the play you told it to play?"

"No," said the Eldest Magician. "That is a new and a bad play."

"Look!" said the Man, and as he spoke the great Sea came up the mouth of the Perak River, driving the river backwards till it overflowed all the dark forests for miles and miles, and flooded the Man's house.

"This is wrong. Launch your canoe and we will find out who is playing with the Sea," said the Eldest Magician. They stepped into the canoe; the little girl-daughter came with them; and the Man took his *kris* — a curving, wavy dagger with a blade like a flame, — and they pushed out on the Perak River. Then the Sea began to run back and back, and the canoe was sucked out of the mouth of the Perak

River, past Selangor, past Malacca, past Singapore, out and out to the Island of Bintang, as though it had been pulled by a string.

Then the Eldest Magician stood up and shouted, "Ho! beasts, birds, and fishes, that I took between my hands at the Very Beginning and taught the play that you should play, which one of you is playing with the Sea?"

Then all the beasts, birds, and fishes said together, "Eldest Magician, we play the plays that you taught us to play — we and our children's children. But not one of us plays with the Sea."

Then the Moon rose big and full over the water, and the Eldest Magician said to the hunchbacked old man who sits in the Moon spinning a fishing-line with which he hopes one day to catch the World, "Ho! Fisher of the Moon, are you playing with the Sea?"

"No," said the Fisherman, "I am spinning a line with which I shall some day catch the World; but I do not play with the Sea." And he went on spinning his line.

Now there is also a Rat up in the Moon who always bites the old Fisherman's line as fast as it is made, and the Eldest Magician said to him, "Ho! Rat of the Moon, are *you* playing with the Sea?"

And the Rat said, "I am too busy biting through the line that this old Fisherman is spinning. I do not play with the Sea." And he went on biting the line.

Then the little girl-daughter put up her little soft brown

arms with the beautiful white shell bracelets and said, "O Eldest Magician! when my father here talked to you at the Very Beginning, and I leaned upon his shoulder while the beasts were being taught their plays, one beast went away naughtily into the Sea before you had taught him his play."

And the Eldest Magician said, "How wise are little children who see and are silent! What was that beast like?"

And the little girl-daughter said, "He was round and he was flat; and his eyes grew upon stalks; and he walked sideways like this; and he was covered with strong armour upon his back."

And the Eldest Magician said, "How wise are little children who speak truth! Now I know where Pau Amma went. Give me the paddle!"

So he took the paddle; but there was no need to paddle, for the water flowed steadily past all the islands till they came to the place called Pusat Tasek — the Heart of the Sea — where the great hollow is that leads down to the heart of the world, and in that hollow grows the Wonderful Tree, Pauh Janggi, that bears the magic twin-nuts. Then the Eldest Magician slid his arm up to the shoulder through the deep warm water, and under the roots of the Wonderful Tree he touched the broad back of Pau Amma the Crab. And Pau Amma settled down at the touch, and all the Sea rose up as water rises in a basin when you put your hand into it.

"Ah!" said the Eldest Magician. "Now I know who has

been playing with the Sea"; and he called out, "What are you doing, Pau Amma?"

And Pau Amma, deep down below, answered, "Once a day and once a night I go out to look for my food. Once a day and once a night I return. Leave me alone."

Then the Eldest Magician said, "Listen, Pau Amma. When you go out from your cave the waters of the Sea pour down into Pusat Tasek, and all the beaches of all the islands are left bare, and the little fish die, and Rajah Moyang Kaban, the King of the Elephants, his legs are made muddy. When you come back and sit in Pusat Tasek, the waters of the Sea rise, and half the little islands are drowned, and the Man's house is flooded, and Rajah Abdullah, the King of the Crocodiles, his mouth is filled with the salt water."

Then Pau Amma, deep down below, laughed and said, "I did not know I was so important. Henceforward I will go out seven times a day, and the waters shall never be still."

And the Eldest Magician said, "I cannot make you play the play you were meant to play, Pau Amma, because you escaped me at the Very Beginning; but if you are not afraid, come up and we will talk about it."

"I am not afraid," said Pau Amma, and he rose to the top of the Sea in the moonlight. There was nobody in the world so big as Pau Amma — for he was the King Crab of all Crabs. Not a common Crab, but a King Crab. One side of his great shell touched the beach at Sarawak; the

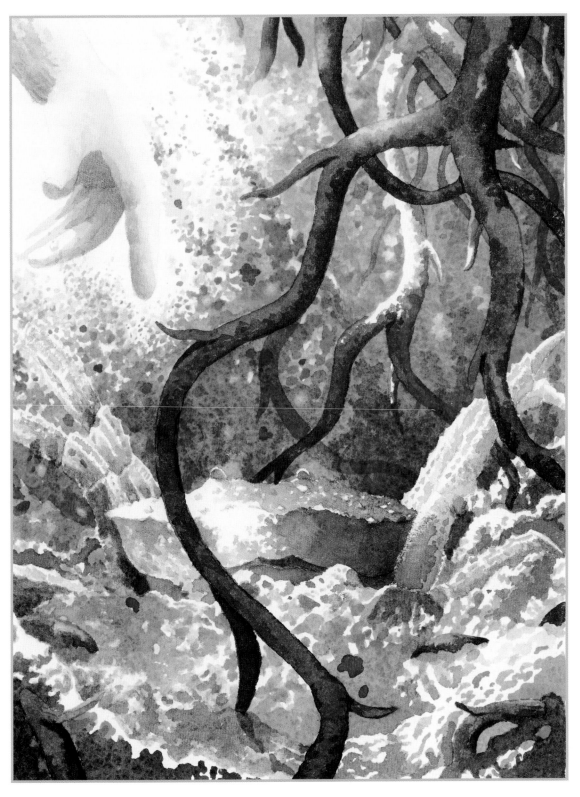

*"Ah," said the Eldest Magician. "Now I know who
has been playing with the Sea."*

"I am not afraid," said Pau Amma, and he rose to the top of the Sea in the moonlight.

other touched the beach at Pahang; and he was taller than the smoke of three volcanoes! As he rose up through the branches of the Wonderful Tree he tore off one of the great twin-fruits — the magic double-kernelled nuts that make people young, — and the little girl-daughter saw it bobbing alongside the canoe, and pulled it in and began to pick out the soft eyes of it with her little golden scissors.

"Now," said the Magician, "make a Magic, Pau Amma, to show that you are really important."

Pau Amma rolled his eyes and waved his legs, but he could only stir up the Sea, because, though he was a King Crab, he was nothing more than a Crab, and the Eldest Magician laughed.

"You are not so important after all, Pau Amma," he said. "Now, let *me* try," and he made a Magic with his left hand — with just the little finger of his left hand — and — lo and behold, Best Beloved, Pau Amma's hard, blue-green-black shell fell off him as a husk falls off a coconut, and Pau Amma was left all soft — soft as the little crabs that you sometimes find on the beach, Best Beloved.

"Indeed, you are very important," said the Eldest Magician. "Shall I ask the Man here to cut you with *kris*? Shall I send for Rajah Moyang Kaban, the King of the Elephants, to pierce you with his tusks? or shall I call Rajah Abdullah, the King of the Crocodiles, to bite you?"

And Pau Amma said, "I am ashamed! Give me back my hard shell and let me go back to Pusat Tasek, and I will only stir out once a day and once a night to get my food."

And the Eldest Magician said, "No, Pau Amma, I will *not* give you back your shell, for you will grow bigger and prouder and stronger, and perhaps you will forget your promise, and you will play with the Sea once more."

Then Pau Amma said, "What shall I do? I am so big that I can only hide in Pusat Tasek, and if I go anywhere else, all soft as I am now, the sharks and the dogfish will eat me. And if I go to Pusat Tasek, all soft as I am now, though I may be safe, I can never stir out to get my food, and so I shall die." Then he waved his legs and lamented.

"Listen, Pau Amma," said the Eldest Magician. "I cannot make you play the play you were meant to play, because you escaped me at the Very Beginning; but if you choose, I can make every stone and every hole and every bunch of weed in all the seas a safe Pusat Tasek for you and your children for always."

Then Pau Amma said, "That is good, but I do not choose yet. Look! there is that Man who talked to you at the Very Beginning. If he had not taken up your attention I should not have grown tired of waiting and run away, and all this would never have happened. What will *he* do for me?"

And the Man said, "If you choose, I will make a Magic, so that both the deep water and the dry ground will be a home for you and your children — so that you shall be able to hide both on the land and in the sea."

And Pau Amma said, "I do not choose yet. Look! there is that girl who saw me running away at the Very Beginning. If she had spoken then, the Eldest Magician would have called me back, and all this would never have happened. What will *she* do for me?"

And the little girl-daughter said, "This is a good nut that I am eating. If you choose, I will make a Magic and I will give you this pair of scissors, very sharp and strong, so that you and your children can eat coconuts like this all day long when you come up from the Sea to the land; or you can dig a Pusat Tasek for yourself with the scissors that belong to you when there is no stone or hole near by; and when the earth is too hard, by the help of these same scissors you can run up a tree."

And Pau Amma said, "I do not choose yet, for, all soft as I am, these gifts would not help me. Give me back my shell, O Eldest Magician, and then I will play your play."

And the Eldest Magician said, "I will give it back, Pau Amma, for eleven months of the year; but on the twelfth month of every year it shall grow soft again, to remind you and all your children that I can make Magics, and to keep you humble, Pau Amma; for I see that if you can run both under the water and on land, you will grow too bold; and if you can climb trees and crack nuts and dig holes with your scissors, you will grow too greedy, Pau Amma."

Then Pau Amma thought a little and said, "I have made my choice. I will take all the gifts."

Then the Eldest Magician made a Magic with the right hand, with all five fingers of his right hand, and lo and behold, Best Beloved, Pau Amma grew smaller and smaller and smaller, till at last there was only a little green crab swimming in the water alongside the canoe, crying in a very small voice, "Give me the scissors!"

And the girl-daughter picked him up on the palm of her little brown hand, and sat him in the bottom of the canoe and gave him her scissors, and he waved them in his little arms, and opened them and shut them and snapped them, and said, "I can eat nuts. I can crack shells. I can dig holes. I can climb trees. I can breathe in the dry air, and I can find a safe Pusat Tasek under every stone. I did not know I was so important. *Kun?* [Is this right?]"

"Payah kun," said the Eldest Magician, and he laughed and gave him his blessing; and little Pau Amma scuttled over the side of the canoe into the water; and he was so tiny that he could have hidden under the shadow of a dry leaf on land or of a dead shell at the bottom of the sea.

"Was that well done?" said the Eldest Magician.

"Yes," said the Man. "But now we must go back to Perak, and that is a weary way to paddle. If we had waited till Pau Amma had gone out of Pusat Tasek and come home, the water would have carried us there by itself."

"You are lazy," said the Eldest Magician. "So your children shall be lazy. They shall be the laziest people in the world. They shall be called the Malazy — the lazy people";

*And he waved them in his little arms, and opened them
and shut them and snapped them.*

and he held up his finger to the Moon and said, "O Fisherman, here is this Man too lazy to row home. Pull his canoe home with your line, Fisherman."

"No," said the Man. "If I am to be lazy all my days, let the Sea work for me twice a day for ever. That will save paddling."

And the Eldest Magician laughed and said, *"Payah kun"* [That is right].

And the Rat of the Moon stopped biting the line; and the Fisherman let his line down till it touched the Sea, and he pulled the whole deep Sea along, past the Island of Bintang, past Singapore, past Malacca, past Selangor, till the canoe whirled into the mouth of the Perak River again.

"Kun?" said the Fisherman of the Moon.

"Payah kun," said the Eldest Magician. "See now that you pull the Sea twice a day and twice a night for ever, so that the Malazy fishermen may be saved paddling. But be careful not to do it too hard, or I shall make a Magic on you as I did to Pau Amma."

Then they all went up the Perak River and went to bed, Best Beloved.

Now listen and attend!

From that day to this the Moon has always pulled the Sea up and down and made what we call the tides. Sometimes the Fisher of the Sea pulls a little too hard, and then we get spring-tides; and sometimes he pulls a little too softly, and then we get what are called neap-tides; but nearly always he is careful, because of the Eldest Magician.

And Pau Amma? You can see when you go to the beach, how all Pau Amma's babies make little Pusat Taseks for themselves under every stone and bunch of weed on the sands; you can see them waving their little scissors; and in some parts of the world they truly live on the dry land and run up the palm-trees and eat coconuts, exactly as the girl-daughter promised. But once a year all Pau Ammas must shake off their hard armour and be soft — to remind them of what the Eldest Magician could do. And so it isn't fair to kill or hunt Pau Amma's babies just because old Pau Amma was stupidly rude a very long time ago.

Oh yes! And Pau Amma's babies hate being taken out of their little Pusat Taseks and brought home in pickle-bottles. That is why they nip you with their scissors, and it serves you right!

CHINA-GOING *P. & O.s*
Pass Pau Amma's playground close,
And his Pusat Tasek lies
Near the track of most B.I.'s.
N.Y.K. and N.D.L.
Know Pau Amma's home as well
As the Fisher of the Sea knows
"Bens," M.M.'s, and Rubattinos.
But (and this is rather queer)
A.T.L.'s can not *come here;*

You can see when you go to the beach, how all Pau Amma's babies
make little Pusat Taseks for themselves.

O. and O. and D.O.A.
Must go round another way.
Orient, Anchor, Bibby, Hall,
Never go that way at all.
U.C.S. would have a fit
If it found itself on it.
And if "Beavers" took their cargoes
To Penang instead of Lagos,
Or a fat Shaw-Savill bore
Passengers to Singapore,
Or a White Star were to try a
Little trip to Sourabaya,
Or a B.S.A. went on
Past Natal to Cheribon,
Then great Mr. Lloyds would come
With a wire and drag them home!

You'll know what my riddle means
When you've eaten mangosteens.

Or if you can't wait till then, ask them to let you have the outside page of the *Times*; turn over to page 2, where it is marked "Shipping" on the top left hand; then take the Atlas (and that is the finest picture-book in the world) and see how the names of the places that the steamers go to fit into the names of the places on the map. Any steamer-kiddy ought to be able to do that; but if you can't read, ask some one to show it you.

THE CAT THAT WALKED
BY HIMSELF

She made the First Singing Magic in the world.

HEAR AND ATTEND and listen; for this befell and behappened and became and was, O my Best Beloved, when the Tame animals were wild. The Dog was wild, and the Horse was wild, and the Cow was wild, and the Sheep was wild, and the Pig was wild — as wild as wild could be — and they walked in the Wet Wild Woods by their wild lones. But the wildest of all the wild animals was the Cat. He walked by himself, and all places were alike to him.

Of course the Man was wild too. He was dreadfully wild. He didn't even begin to be tame till he met the Woman, and she told him that she did not like living in his wild ways. She picked out a nice dry Cave, instead of a heap of wet leaves, to lie down in; and she strewed clean sand on the floor; and she lit a nice fire of wood at the back of the Cave; and she hung a dried wild-horse skin, tail-down, across the opening of the Cave; and she said, "Wipe your feet, dear, when you come in, and now we'll keep house."

That night, Best Beloved, they ate wild sheep roasted on the hot stones, and flavoured with wild garlic and wild pepper; and wild duck stuffed with wild rice and wild fenugreek and wild coriander; and marrow-bones of wild oxen; and wild cherries, and wild grenadillas. Then the Man went to sleep in front of the fire ever so happy; but the Woman sat up, combing her hair. She took the bone of the shoulder of mutton — the big fat blade-bone — and she looked at the wonderful marks on it, and she threw more wood on the fire, and she made a Magic. She made the First Singing Magic in the world.

Out in the Wet Wild Woods all the wild animals gathered together where they could see the light of the fire a long way off, and they wondered what it meant.

Then Wild Horse stamped with his wild foot and said, "O my Friends and O my Enemies, why have the Man and the Woman made that great light in that great Cave, and what harm will it do us?"

Wild Dog lifted up his wild nose and smelled the smell of the roast mutton, and said, "I will go up and see and look, and say; for I think it is good. Cat, come with me."

"Nenni!" said the Cat. "I am the Cat who walks by himself, and all places are alike to me. I will not come."

"Then we can never be friends again," said Wild Dog, and he trotted off to the Cave. But when he had gone a little way the Cat said to himself, "All places are alike to me. Why should I not go too and see and look and come away at my own liking." So he slipped after Wild Dog softly, very softly, and hid himself where he could hear everything.

When Wild Dog reached the mouth of the Cave he

lifted up the dried horse-skin with his nose and sniffed the beautiful smell of the roast mutton, and the Woman, looking at the blade-bone, heard him, and laughed, and said, "Here comes the first. Wild Thing out of the Wild Woods, what do you want?"

Wild Dog said, "O my Enemy and Wife of my Enemy, what is this that smells so good in the Wild Woods?"

Then the Woman picked up a roasted mutton-bone and threw it to Wild Dog, and said, "Wild Thing out of the Wild Woods, taste and try." Wild Dog gnawed the bone, and it was more delicious than anything he had ever tasted, and he said, "O my Enemy and Wife of my Enemy, give me another."

The Woman said, "Wild Thing out of the Wild Woods, help my Man to hunt through the day and guard this Cave at night, and I will give you as many roast bones as you need."

"Ah!" said the Cat, listening. "This is a very wise Woman, but she is not so wise as I am."

Wild Dog crawled into the Cave and laid his head on the Woman's lap, and said, "O my Friend and Wife of my Friend, I will help Your Man to hunt through the day, and at night I will guard your Cave."

"Ah!" said the Cat, listening. "That is a very foolish Dog." And he went back through the Wet Wild Woods waving his wild tail, and walking by his wild lone. But he never told anybody.

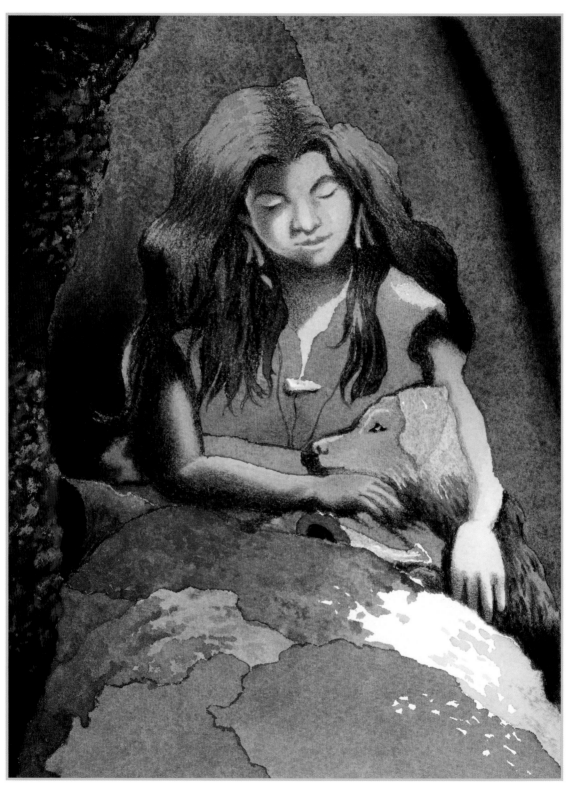

"O my Friend and Wife of my Friend, I will help Your Man to
hunt through the day, and at night I will guard your Cave."

When the Man waked up he said, "What is Wild Dog doing here?" And the Woman said, "His name is not Wild Dog any more, but the First Friend, because he will be our friend for always and always and always. Take him with you when you go hunting."

Next night the Woman cut great green armfuls of fresh grass from the water-meadows, and dried it before the fire, so that it smelt like new-mown hay, and she sat at the mouth of the Cave and plaited a halter out of horse-hide, and she looked at the shoulder-of-mutton bone — at the big broad blade-bone — and she made a Magic. She made the Second Singing Magic in the world.

Out in the Wild Woods all the wild animals wondered what had happened to Wild Dog, and at last Wild Horse stamped with his foot and said, "I will go and see and say why Wild Dog has not returned. Cat, come with me."

"Nenni!" said the Cat. "I am the Cat who walks by himself, and all places are alike to me. I will not come." But all the same he followed Wild Horse softly, very softly, and hid himself where he could hear everything.

When the Woman heard Wild Horse tripping and stumbling on his long mane, she laughed and said, "Here comes the second. Wild Thing out of the Wild Woods, what do you want?"

Wild Horse said, "O my Enemy and Wife of my Enemy, where is Wild Dog?"

The Woman laughed, and picked up the blade-bone

and looked at it, and said, "Wild Thing out of the Wild Woods, you did not come here for Wild Dog, but for the sake of this good grass."

And Wild Horse, tripping and stumbling on his long mane, said, "That is true; give it me to eat."

The Woman said, "Wild Thing out of the Wild Woods, bend your wild head and wear what I give you, and you shall eat the wonderful grass three times a day."

"Ah," said the Cat, listening. "This is a clever Woman, but she is not so clever as I am."

Wild Horse bent his wild head, and the Woman slipped the plaited-hide halter over it, and Wild Horse breathed on the Woman's feet and said, "O my Mistress, and Wife of my Master, I will be your servant for the sake of the wonderful grass."

"Ah," said the Cat, listening. "That is a very foolish Horse." And he went back through the Wet Wild Woods, waving his wild tail and walking by his wild lone. But he never told anybody.

When the Man and the Dog came back from hunting, the Man said, "What is Wild Horse doing here?" And the Woman said, "His name is not Wild Horse any more, but the First Servant, because he will carry us from place to place for always and always and always. Ride on his back when you go hunting."

Next day, holding her wild head high that her wild horns should not catch in the wild trees, Wild Cow came

Wild Horse bent his wild head, and the Woman slipped the
plaited-hide halter over it.

up to the Cave, and the Cat followed, and hid himself just the same as before; and everything happened just the same as before; and the Cat said the same things as before; and when Wild Cow had promised to give her milk to the Woman every day in exchange for the wonderful grass, the Cat went back through the Wet Wild Woods waving his wild tail and walking by his wild lone, just the same as before. But he never told anybody. And when the Man and the Horse and the Dog came home from hunting and asked the same questions same as before, the Woman said, "Her name is not Wild Cow any more, but the Giver of Good Food. She will give us the warm white milk for always and always and always, and I will take care of her while you and the First Friend and the First Servant go hunting."

Next day the Cat waited to see if any other Wild Thing would go up to the Cave, but no one moved in the Wet Wild Woods, so the Cat walked there by himself; and he saw the Woman milking the Cow, and he saw the light of the fire in the Cave, and he smelt the smell of the warm white milk.

Cat said, "O my Enemy and Wife of my Enemy, where did Wild Cow go?"

The Woman laughed and said, "Wild Thing out of the Wild Woods, go back to the Woods again, for I have braided up my hair, and I have put away the magic blade-bone, and we have no more need of either friends or servants in our Cave."

Cat said, "I am not a friend, and I am not a servant. I am the Cat who walks by himself, and I wish to come into your Cave."

Woman said, "Then why did you not come with First Friend on the first night?"

Cat grew very angry and said, "Has Wild Dog told tales of me?"

Then the Woman laughed and said, "You are the Cat who walks by himself, and all places are alike to you. You are neither a friend nor a servant. You have said it yourself. Go away and walk by yourself in all places alike."

Then Cat pretended to be sorry and said, "Must I never come into the Cave? Must I never sit by the warm fire? Must I never drink the warm white milk? You are very wise and very beautiful. You should not be cruel even to a Cat."

Woman said, "I knew I was wise, but I did not know I was beautiful. So I will make a bargain with you. If ever I say one word in your praise, you may come into the Cave."

"And if you say two words in my praise?" said the Cat.

"I never shall," said the Woman, "but if I say two words in your praise, you may sit by the fire in the Cave."

"And if you say three words?" said the Cat.

"I never shall," said the Woman, "but if I say three words in your praise, you may drink the warm white milk three times a day for always and always and always."

Then the Cat arched his back and said, "Now let the Curtain at the mouth of the Cave, and the Fire at the back of the Cave, and the Milk-pots that stand beside the Fire, remember what my Enemy and the Wife of my Enemy has said." And he went away through the Wet Wild Woods waving his wild tail and walking by his wild lone.

That night when the Man and the Horse and the Dog came home from hunting, the Woman did not tell them of the bargain that she had made with the Cat, because she was afraid that they might not like it.

Cat went far and far away and hid himself in the Wet Wild Woods by his wild lone for a long time till the Woman forgot all about him. Only the Bat — the little upside-down Bat — that hung inside the Cave knew where Cat hid; and every evening Bat would fly to Cat with news of what was happening.

One evening Bat said, "There is a Baby in the Cave. He is new and pink and fat and small, and the Woman is very fond of him."

"Ah," said the Cat, listening. "But what is the Baby fond of?"

"He is fond of things that are soft and tickle," said the Bat. "He is fond of warm things to hold in his arms when he goes to sleep. He is fond of being played with. He is fond of all those things."

"Ah!" said the Cat, listening. "Then my time has come."

Next night Cat walked through the Wet Wild Woods and hid very near the Cave till morning-time, and Man and Dog and Horse went hunting. The Woman was busy

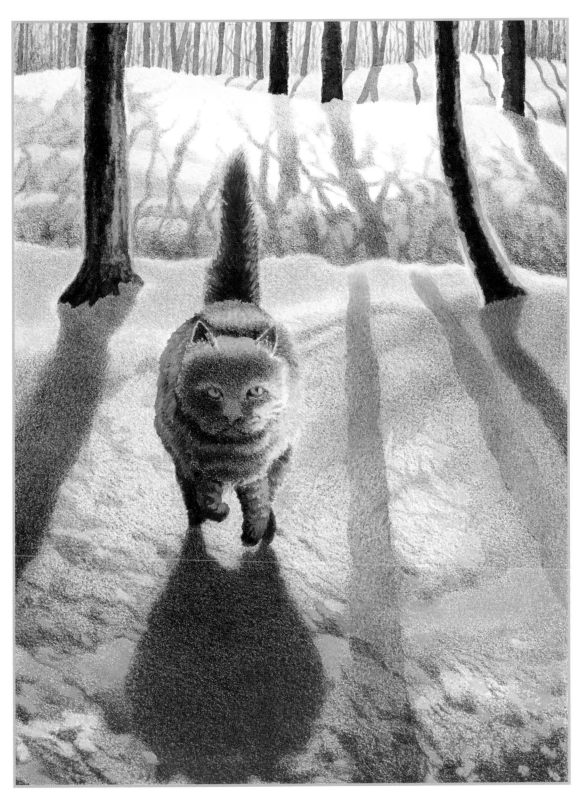

*Cat went far and far away and hid himself in
the Wet Wild Woods.*

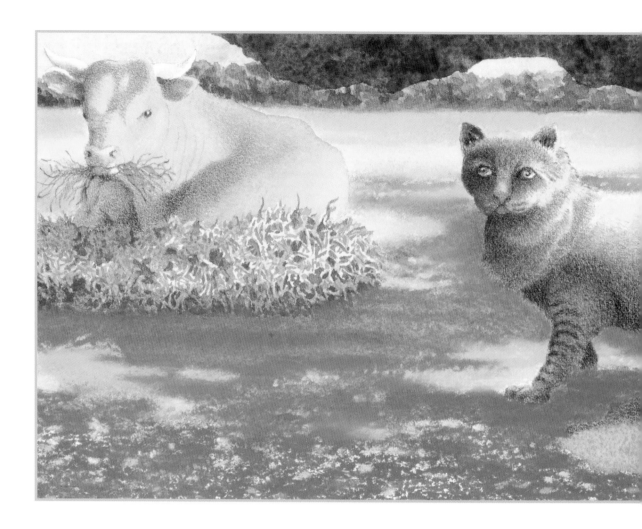

cooking that morning, and the Baby cried and interrupted. So she carried him outside the Cave and gave him a handful of pebbles to play with. But still the Baby cried.

Then the Cat put out his paddy paw and patted the Baby on the cheek, and it cooed; and the Cat rubbed against its fat knees and tickled it under its fat chin with his tail. And the Baby laughed; and the Woman heard him and smiled.

Then the Bat — the little upside-down Bat — that hung

in the mouth of the Cave said, "O my Hostess and Wife of my Host and Mother of my Host's Son, a Wild Thing from the Wild Woods is most beautifully playing with your Baby."

The Cat tickled it under its fat chin with his tail.

"A blessing on that Wild Thing whoever he may be," said the Woman, straightening her back, "for I was a busy woman this morning and he has done me a service."

That very minute and second, Best Beloved, the dried horse-skin Curtain that was stretched tail-down at the mouth of the Cave fell down — *woosh!* — because it re-membered the bargain she had made with the Cat; and when the Woman went to pick it up — lo and behold! — the Cat was sitting quite comfy inside the Cave.

"O my Enemy and Wife of my Enemy and Mother of my Enemy," said the Cat, "it is I: for you have spoken a word in my praise, and now I can sit within the Cave for always and always and always. But still I am the Cat who walks by himself, and all places are alike to me."

The Woman was very angry, and shut her lips tight and took up her spinning-wheel and began to spin.

But the Baby cried because the Cat had gone away, and the Woman could not hush it, for it struggled and kicked and grew black in the face.

"O my Enemy and Wife of my Enemy and Mother of my Enemy," said the Cat, "take a strand of the thread that you are spinning and tie it to your spindle-whorl and drag it along the floor, and I will show you a Magic that shall make your Baby laugh as loudly as he is now crying."

"I will do so," said the Woman, "because I am at my wits' end; but I will not thank you for it."

She tied the thread to the little clay spindle-whorl and drew it across the floor, and the Cat ran after it and patted it with his paws and rolled head over heels, and tossed it backward over his shoulder and chased it between his hind-legs and pretended to lose it, and pounced down upon it again, till the Baby laughed as loudly as it had been crying, and scrambled after the Cat and frolicked all over the Cave till it grew tired and settled down to sleep with the Cat in its arms.

"Now," said Cat, "I will sing the Baby a song that shall keep him asleep for an hour." And he began to purr, loud and low, low and loud, till the Baby fell fast asleep. The Woman smiled as she looked down upon the two of them, and said, "That was wonderfully done. No question but you are very clever, O Cat."

That very minute and second, Best Beloved, the smoke of the fire at the back of the Cave came down in clouds from the roof — *puff!* — because it remembered the bargain she had made with the Cat; and when it had cleared away — lo and behold! — the Cat was sitting quite comfy close to the fire.

"O my Enemy and Wife of my Enemy and Mother of my Enemy," said the Cat, "it is I: for you have spoken a second word in my praise, and now I can sit by the warm fire at the back of the Cave for always and always and always. But still I am the Cat who walks by himself, and all places are alike to me."

Then the Woman was very very angry, and let down her hair and put more wood on the fire and brought out the broad blade-bone of the shoulder of mutton and began to make a Magic that should prevent her from saying a third word in praise of the Cat. It was not a Singing Magic, Best Beloved, it was a Still Magic; and by and by the Cave

The Cat was lapping up the warm white milk that lay in one of the broken pieces.

grew so still that a little wee-wee mouse crept out of a corner and ran across the floor.

"O my Enemy and Wife of my Enemy and Mother of my Enemy," said the Cat, "is that little mouse part of your Magic?"

"Ouh! Chee! No indeed!" said the Woman, and she dropped the blade-bone and jumped upon the footstool in front of the fire and braided up her hair very quick for fear that the mouse should run up it.

"Ah," said the Cat, watching. "Then the mouse will do me no harm if I eat it?"

"No," said the Woman, braiding up her hair, "eat it quickly and I will ever be grateful to you."

Cat made one jump and caught the little mouse, and the Woman said, "A hundred thanks. Even the First Friend is not quick enough to catch little mice as you have done. You must be very wise."

That very minute and second, O Best Beloved, the Milk-pot that stood by the fire cracked in two pieces — *ffft!* — because it remembered the bargain she had made with the Cat; and when the Woman jumped down from the footstool — lo and behold! — the Cat was lapping up the warm white milk that lay in one of the broken pieces.

"O my Enemy and Wife of my Enemy and Mother of my Enemy," said the Cat, "it is I: for you have spoken three words in my praise, and now I can drink the warm white milk three times a day for always and always and always. But *still* I am the Cat who walks by himself, and all places are alike to me."

Then the Woman laughed and set the Cat a bowl of the warm white milk and said, "O Cat, you are as clever as a man, but remember that your bargain was not made with the Man or the Dog, and I do not know what they will do when they come home."

"What is that to me?" said the Cat. "If I have my place in the Cave by the fire and my warm white milk three times a day I do not care what the Man or the Dog can do."

That evening when the Man and the Dog came into the Cave, the Woman told them all the story of the bargain, while the Cat sat by the fire and smiled. Then the Man said, "Yes, but he has not made a bargain with *me* or with all proper Men after me." Then he took off his two leather boots and he took up his little stone axe (that makes three) and he fetched a piece of wood and a hatchet (that is five altogether), and he set them out in a row and he said, "Now we will make *our* bargain. If you do not catch mice when you are in the Cave for always and always and always, I will throw these five things at you whenever I see you, and so shall all proper Men do after me."

"Ah," said the Woman, listening. "This is a very clever Cat, but he is not so clever as my Man."

The Cat counted the five things (and they looked very knobby) and he said, "I will catch mice when I am in the

Cave for always and always and always; but *still* I am the Cat who walks by himself, and all places are alike to me."

"Not when I am near," said the Man. "If you had not said that last I would have put all these things away for always and always and always; but now I am going to throw my two boots and my little stone axe (that makes three) at you whenever I meet you. And so shall all proper Men do after me!"

Then the Dog said, "Wait a minute. He has not made a bargain with *me* or with all proper Dogs after me." And he showed his teeth and said, "If you are not kind to the Baby while I am in the Cave for always and always and always, I will hunt you till I catch you, and when I catch you I will bite you. And so shall all proper Dogs do after me."

"Ah," said the Woman, listening. "This is a very clever Cat, but he is not so clever as the Dog."

Cat counted the Dog's teeth (and they looked very pointed) and he said, "I will be kind to the Baby while I am in the Cave, as long as he does not pull my tail too hard, for always and always and always. But *still* I am the Cat who walks by himself, and all places are alike to me!"

"Not when I am near," said the Dog. "If you had not said that last I would have shut my mouth for always and always and always; but *now* I am going to hunt you up a tree whenever I meet you. And so shall all proper Dogs do after me."

Then the Man threw his two boots and his little stone

axe (that makes three) at the Cat, and the Cat ran out of the Cave and the Dog chased him up a tree; and from that day to this, Best Beloved, three proper Men out of five will always throw things at a Cat whenever they meet him, and all proper Dogs will chase him up a tree. But the Cat keeps his side of the bargain too. He will kill mice, and he will be kind to Babies when he is in the house, just as long as they do not pull his tail too hard. But when he has done that, and between times, and when the moon gets up and night comes, he is the Cat that walks by himself, and all places are alike to him. Then he goes out to the Wet Wild Woods or up the Wet Wild Trees or on the Wet Wild Roofs, waving his wild tail and walking by his wild lone.

> Pussy can *sit by the fire and sing,*
>   *Pussy can climb a tree,*
> *Or play with a silly old cork and string*
>   *To 'muse herself, not me.*
> *But I like* Binkie *my dog, because*
>   *He knows how to behave;*
> *So,* Binkie's *the same as the First Friend was,*
>   *And I am the Man in the Cave!*

> *Pussy will play Man Friday till*
>   *It's time to wet her paw*
> *And make her walk on the window-sill*
>   *(For the footprint Crusoe saw);*

Then she fluffles her tail and mews,
And scratches and won't attend.
But Binkie *will play whatever I choose,*
And he is my true First Friend.

Pussy will rub my knees with her head
Pretending she loves me hard;
But the very minute I go to my bed
Pussy runs out in the yard,
And there she stays till the morning-light;
So I know it is only pretend;
But Binkie, *he snores at my feet all night,*
And he is my Firstest Friend!

THE BUTTERFLY
THAT STAMPED

He understood what the beasts said, what the birds said,
what the fishes said, and what the insects said.

THIS, O MY BEST BELOVED, is a story — a new and a wonderful story — a story quite different from the other stories — a story about The Most Wise Sovereign Suleiman-bin-Daoud — Solomon the Son of David.

There are three hundred and fifty-five stories about Suleiman-bin-Daoud; but this is not one of them. It is not the story of the Lapwing who found the Water; or the Hoopoe who shaded Suleiman-bin-Daoud from the heat. It is not the story of the Glass Pavement, or the Ruby with the Crooked Hole, or the Gold Bars of Balkis. It is the story of the Butterfly that Stamped.

Now attend all over again and listen!

Suleiman-bin-Daoud was wise. He understood what the beasts said, what the birds said, what the fishes said, and what the insects said. He understood what the rocks said deep under the earth when they bowed in towards each other and groaned; and he understood what the trees said when they rustled in the middle of the morning. He understood everything, from the bishop on the bench to the hyssop on the wall; and Balkis, his Head Queen, the

Most Beautiful Queen Balkis, was nearly as wise as he was.

Suleiman-bin-Daoud was strong. Upon the third finger of his right hand he wore a ring. When he turned it once, Afrits and Djinns came out of the earth to do whatever he told them. When he turned it twice, Fairies came down from the sky to do whatever he told them; and when he turned it three times, the very great angel Azrael of the Sword came dressed as a water-carrier, and told him the news of the three worlds, — Above — Below — and Here.

And yet Suleiman-bin-Daoud was not proud. He very seldom showed off, and when he did he was sorry for it. Once he tried to feed all the animals in all the world in one day, but when the food was ready an Animal came out of the deep sea and ate it up in three mouthfuls. Suleiman-bin-Daoud was very surprised and said, "O Animal, who are you?" And the Animal said, "O King, live forever! I am the smallest of thirty thousand brothers, and our home is at the bottom of the sea. We heard that you were going to feed all the animals in all the world, and my brothers sent me to ask when dinner would be ready." Suleiman-bin-Daoud was more surprised than ever and said, "O Animal, you have eaten all the dinner that I made ready for all the animals in the world." And the Animal said, "O King, live for ever, but do you really call *that* a dinner? Where I come from we each eat twice as much as that between meals." Then Suleiman-bin-Daoud fell flat on his face and said, "O Animal! I gave that dinner to show what a great and rich king I was, and not because I really wanted to be kind to the animals. Now I am ashamed, and it serves me right." Suleiman-bin-Daoud was a really truly wise man, Best Beloved. After that he never forgot that it was silly to show off; and now the real story part of my story begins.

He married ever so many wives. He married nine hundred and ninety-nine wives, besides the Most Beautiful Balkis; and they all lived in a great golden palace in the middle of a lovely garden with fountains. He didn't really want nine-hundred and ninety-nine wives, but in those days everybody married ever so many wives, and of course the King had to marry ever so many more just to show that he was the King.

Some of the wives were nice, but some were simply horrid, and the horrid ones quarrelled with the nice ones and made them horrid too, and then they would all quarrel with Suleiman-bin-Daoud, and that was horrid for him. But Balkis the Most Beautiful never quarrelled with Suleiman-bin-Daoud. She loved him too much. She sat in her rooms in the Golden Palace, or walked in the Palace garden, and was truly sorry for him.

Of course if he had chosen to turn his ring on his finger and call up the Djinns and the Afrits they would have magicked all those nine hundred and ninety-nine quarrelsome wives into white mules of the desert or greyhounds or pomegranate seeds; but Suleiman-bin-Daoud thought that that would be showing off. So, when they quarrelled too much, he only walked by himself in one part of the beautiful Palace gardens and wished he had never been born.

One day, when they had quarrelled for three weeks — all nine hundred and ninety-nine wives together — Suleiman-bin-Daoud went out for peace and quiet as usual; and among the orange trees he met Balkis the Most Beautiful, very sorrowful because Suleiman-bin-Daoud was so worried. And she said to him, "O my Lord and Light of my Eyes, turn the ring upon your finger and show these Queens of Egypt and Mesopotamia and Persia and China that you are the great and terrible King." But Suleiman-bin-Daoud shook his head and said, "O my Lady and Delight of my Life, remember the Animal that came out of the sea and made me ashamed before all the animals in all the world because I showed off. Now, if I showed off before these Queens of Persia and Egypt and Abyssinia and China, merely because they worry me, I might be made even more ashamed than I have been."

And Balkis the Most Beautiful said, "O my Lord and Treasure of my Soul, what will you do?"

And Suleiman-bin-Daoud said, "O my Lady and Content of my Heart, I shall continue to endure my fate at the hands of these nine hundred and ninety-nine Queens who vex me with their continual quarrelling."

So he went on between the lilies and the loquats and the roses and the cannas and the heavy-scented ginger-plants that grew in the garden, till he came to the great camphor-

*"O my Lady and Content of my Heart, I shall continue
to endure my fate."*

tree that was called the Camphor-Tree of Suleiman-bin-Daoud. But Balkis hid among the tall irises and the spotted bamboos and the red lilies behind the camphor-tree, so as to be near her own true love, Suleiman-bin-Daoud.

Presently two Butterflies flew under the tree, quarrelling.

Suleiman-bin-Daoud heard one say to the other, "I wonder at your presumption in talking like this to me. Don't you know that if I stamped with my foot all Suleiman-bin-Daoud's Palace and this garden here would immediately vanish in a clap of thunder?"

Then Suleiman-bin-Daoud forgot his nine hundred and ninety-nine bothersome wives, and laughed, till the camphor-tree shook, at the Butterfly's boast. And he held out his finger and said, "Little man, come here."

The Butterfly was dreadfully frightened, but he managed to fly up to the hand of Suleiman-bin-Daoud, and clung there, fanning himself. Suleiman-bin-Daoud bent his head and whispered very softly, "Little man, you know that all your stamping wouldn't bend one blade of grass. What made you tell that awful fib to your wife? — for doubtless she is your wife."

The Butterfly looked at Suleiman-bin-Daoud and saw the most wise King's eyes twinkle like stars on a frosty night, and he picked up his courage with both wings, and he put his head on one side and said, "O King, live for ever. She *is* my wife; and you know what wives are like."

Suleiman-bin-Daoud smiled in his beard and said, "Yes, *I* know, little brother."

"One must keep them in order somehow," said the Butterfly, "and she has been quarrelling with me all the morning. I said that to quiet her."

And Suleiman-bin-Daoud said, "May it quiet her. Go back to your wife, little brother, and let me hear what you say."

Back flew the Butterfly to his wife, who was all of a twitter behind a leaf, and she said, "He heard you! Suleiman-bin-Daoud himself heard you!"

"Heard me!" said the Butterfly. "Of course he did. I meant him to hear me."

"And what did he say? Oh, what did he say?"

"Well," said the Butterfly, fanning himself most importantly, "between you and me, my dear — of course I don't blame him, because his Palace must have cost a great deal and the oranges are just ripening, — he asked me not to stamp, and I promised I wouldn't."

"Gracious!" said his wife, and sat quite quiet; but Suleiman-bin-Daoud laughed till the tears ran down his face at the impudence of the bad little Butterfly.

Balkis the Most Beautiful stood up behind the tree among the red lilies and smiled to herself, for she had heard all this talk. She thought, "If I am wise I can yet save my Lord from the persecutions of these quarrelsome Queens," and she held out her finger and whispered softly to the Butterfly's Wife, "Little woman, come here."

Up flew the Butterfly's Wife, very frightened, and clung to Balkis's white hand.

Balkis bent her beautiful head down and whispered, "Little woman, do you believe what your husband has just said?"

The Butterfly's Wife looked at Balkis, and saw the Most Beautiful Queen's eyes shining like deep pools with starlight on them, and she picked up her courage with both wings and said, "O Queen, be lovely for ever! *You* know what men-folk are like."

And the Queen Balkis, the Wise Balkis of Sheba, put her hand to her lips to hide a smile and said, "Little sister, *I* know."

"They get angry," said the Butterfly's Wife, fanning herself quickly, "over nothing at all, but we must humour them, O Queen. They never mean half they say. If it pleases my husband to believe that I believe he can make Suleiman-bin-Daoud's Palace disappear by stamping his foot, I'm sure *I* don't care. He'll forget all about it tomorrow."

"Little sister," said Balkis, "you are quite right; but next time he begins to boast, take him at his word. Ask him to stamp, and see what will happen. *We* know what men-folk are like, don't we? He'll be very much ashamed."

Away flew the Butterfly's Wife to her husband, and in five minutes they were quarrelling worse than ever.

"Remember!" said the Butterfly. "Remember what I can do if I stamp my foot."

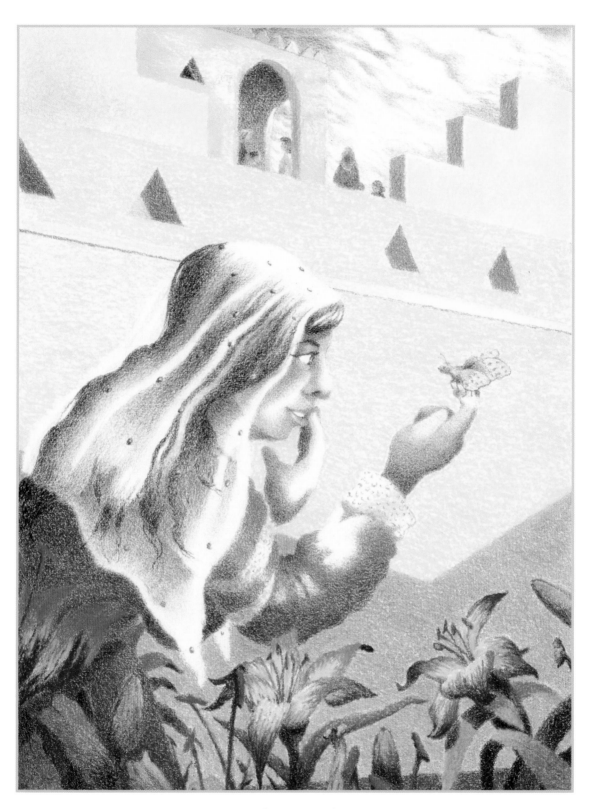

"Little Sister, I know."

"I don't believe you one little bit," said the Butterfly's Wife. "I should very much like to see it done. Suppose you stamp now."

"I promised Suleiman-bin-Daoud that I wouldn't," said the Butterfly, "and I don't want to break my promise."

"It wouldn't matter if you did," said his wife. "You couldn't bend a blade of grass with your stamping. I dare you to do it," she said. "Stamp! Stamp! Stamp!"

Suleiman-bin-Daoud, sitting under the camphor-tree, heard every word of this, and he laughed as he had never laughed in his life before. He forgot all about his Queens; he forgot about the Animal that came out of the sea; he forgot about showing off. He just laughed with joy, and Balkis, on the other side of the tree, smiled because her own true love was so joyful.

Presently the Butterfly, very hot and puffy, came whirling back under the shadow of the camphor-tree and said to Suleiman, "She wants me to stamp! She wants to see what will happen, O Suleiman-bin-Daoud! You know I can't do it, and now she'll never believe a word I say. She'll laugh at me to the end of my days!"

"No, little brother," said Suleiman-bin-Daoud, "she will never laugh at you again," and he turned the ring on his finger — just for the little Butterfly's sake, not for the sake of showing off, — and, lo and behold, four huge Djinns came out of the earth!

"Slaves," said Suleiman-bin-Daoud, "when this gentleman on my finger" (that was where the impudent Butterfly was sitting) "stamps his left front forefoot you will make my Palace and these gardens disappear in a clap of thunder. When he stamps again you will bring them back carefully."

"Now, little brother," he said, "go back to your wife and stamp all you've a mind to."

Away flew the Butterfly to his wife, who was crying, "I dare you to do it! I dare you to do it! Stamp! Stamp now! Stamp!" Balkis saw the four vast Djinns stoop down to the four corners of the gardens with the Palace in the middle, and she clapped her hands softly and said, "At last Sulei-man-bin-Daoud will do for the sake of a Butterfly what he ought to have done long ago for his own sake, and the quarrelsome Queens will be frightened!"

Then the Butterfly stamped. The Djinns jerked the Palace and the gardens a thousand miles into the air: there was a most awful thunder-clap, and everything grew inky black. The Butterfly's Wife fluttered about in the dark, cry-ing, "Oh, I'll be good! I'm so sorry I spoke! Only bring the gardens back, my dear darling husband, and I'll never contradict again."

The Butterfly was nearly as frightened as his wife, and Suleiman-bin-Daoud laughed so much that it was several minutes before he found breath enough to whisper to the Butterfly, "Stamp again, little brother. Give me back my Palace, most great magician."

"Yes, give him back his Palace," said the Butterfly's Wife,

The Djinns jerked the Palace and the gardens
a thousand miles into the air.

still flying about in the dark like a moth. "Give him back his Palace, and don't let's have any more horrid magic."

"Well, my dear," said the Butterfly as bravely as he could, "you see what your nagging has led to. Of course it doesn't make any difference to *me* — I'm used to this kind of thing — but as a favour to you and to Suleiman-bin-Daoud I don't mind putting things right."

So he stamped once more, and that instant the Djinns let down the Palace and the gardens, without even a bump. The sun shone on the dark-green orange-leaves; the fountains played among the pink Egyptian lilies; the birds went on singing; and the Butterfly's Wife lay on her side under the camphor-tree waggling her wings and panting, "Oh, I'll be good! I'll be good!"

Suleiman-bin-Daoud could hardly speak for laughing. He leaned back all weak and hiccupy, and shook his finger at the Butterfly and said, "O great wizard, what is the sense of returning to me my Palace if at the same time you slay me with mirth?"

Then came a terrible noise, for all the nine hundred and ninety-nine Queens ran out of the Palace shrieking and shouting and calling for their babies. They hurried down the great marble steps below the fountain, one hundred abreast, and the Most Wise Balkis went statelily forward to meet them and said, "What is your trouble, O Queens?"

They stood on the marble steps one hundred abreast and shouted, "*What* is our trouble? We were living peacefully in our golden Palace, as is our custom, when upon a sudden the Palace disappeared, and we were left sitting in a thick and noisome darkness; and it thundered, and Djinns and Afrits moved about in the darkness! *That* is our trouble, O Head Queen, and we are most extremely troubled on account of that trouble, for it was a troublesome trouble, unlike any trouble we have known."

Then Balkis the Most Beautiful Queen — Suleiman-bin-Daoud's Very Best Beloved — Queen that was of Sheba and Sabie and the Rivers of the Gold of the South — from the Desert of Zinn to the Towers of Zimbabwe — Balkis, almost as wise as the Most Wise Suleiman-bin-Daoud himself, said, "It is nothing, O Queens! A Butterfly has made complaint against his wife because she quarrelled with him, and it has pleased our Lord Suleiman-bin-Daoud to teach her a lesson in low-speaking and humbleness, for that is counted a virtue among the wives of the butterflies."

Then up and spoke an Egyptian Queen — the daughter of a Pharaoh — and she said, "Our Palace cannot be plucked up by the roots like a leek for the sake of a little insect. No! Suleiman-bin-Daoud must be dead, and what we heard and saw was the earth thundering and darkening at the news."

Then Balkis beckoned that bold Queen without looking at her, and said to her and to the others, "Come and see."

They came down the marble steps, one hundred abreast, and beneath his camphor-tree, still weak with laughing,

"What is your trouble, O Queens?"

they saw the Most Wise King Suleiman-bin-Daoud rocking back and forth with a Butterfly on either hand, and they heard him say, "O wife of my brother in the air, remember after this to please your husband in all things, lest he be provoked to stamp his foot yet again; for he has said that he is used to this Magic, and he is most eminently a great magician — one who steals away the very Palace of Suleiman-bin-Daoud himself. Go in peace, little folk!" And he kissed them on the wings, and they flew away.

Then all the Queens except Balkis — the Most Beautiful and Splendid Balkis, who stood apart smiling — fell flat on their faces, for they said, "If these things are done when a Butterfly is displeased with his wife, what shall be done to us who have vexed our King with our loud-speaking and open quarrelling through many days?"

Then they put their veils over their heads, and they put their hands over their mouths, and they tiptoed back to the Palace most mousy-quiet.

Then Balkis — the Most Beautiful and Excellent Balkis — went forward through the red lilies into the shade of the camphor-tree and laid her hand upon Suleiman-bin-Daoud's shoulder and said, "O my Lord and Treasure of my Soul, rejoice, for we have taught the Queens of Egypt and Mesopotamia and Abyssinia and Persia and India and China with a great and a memorable teaching."

And Suleiman-bin-Daoud, still looking after the Butterflies where they played in the sunlight, said, "O my

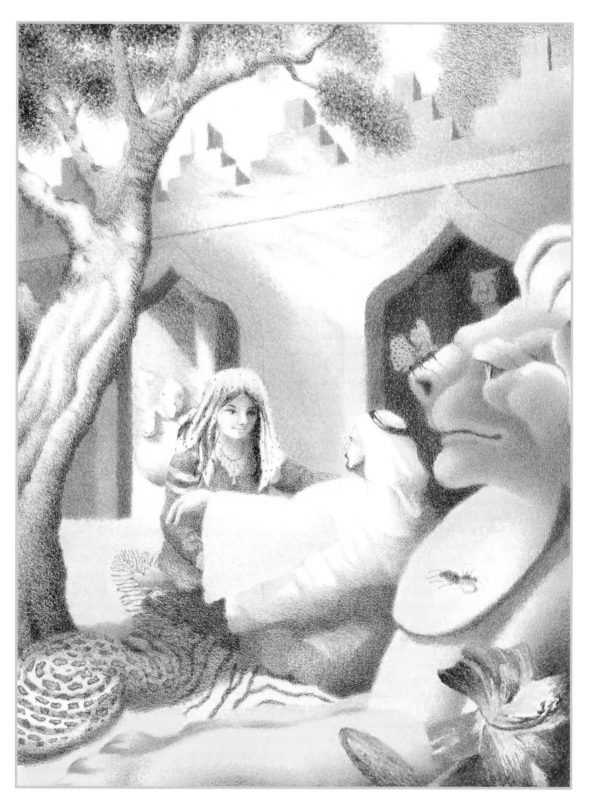

"O my Lord and Treasure of my Soul, rejoice."

Lady and Jewel of my Felicity, when did this happen? For I have been jesting with a Butterfly ever since I came into the garden." And he told Balkis what he had done.

Balkis — the Tender and Most Lovely Balkis — said, "O my Lord and Regent of my Existence, I hid behind the camphor-tree and saw it all. It was I who told the Butterfly's Wife to ask the Butterfly to stamp, because I hoped that for the sake of the jest my Lord would make some great Magic and that the Queens would see it and be frightened." And she told him what the Queens had said and seen and thought.

Then Suleiman-bin-Daoud rose up from his seat under the camphor-tree, and stretched his arms and rejoiced and said, "O my Lady and Sweetener of my Days, know that if I had made a Magic against my Queens for the sake of pride or anger, as I made that feast for all the animals, I should certainly have been put to shame. But by means of your wisdom I made the Magic for the sake of a jest and for the sake of a little Butterfly, and — behold — it has also delivered me from the vexations of my vexatious wives! Tell me, therefore, O my Lady and Heart of my Heart, how did you come to be so wise?"

And Balkis the Queen, beautiful and tall, looked up into Suleiman-bin-Daoud's eyes and put her head a little on one side, just like the Butterfly, and said, "First, O my Lord, because I loved you; and secondly, O my Lord, because I know what women-folk are."

Then they went up to the Palace and lived happily ever afterwards.

But wasn't it clever of Balkis?

> THERE WAS *never a Queen like Balkis,*
>   *From here to the wide world's end;*
> *But Balkis talked to a butterfly*
>   *As you would talk to a friend.*
>
> *There was never a King like Solomon,*
>   *Not since the world began;*
> *But Solomon talked to a butterfly*
>   *As a man would talk to a man.*
>
> She *was Queen of Sabaea —*
>   *And* he *was Asia's Lord —*
> *But they both of 'em talked to butterflies*
>   *When they took their walks abroad!*

ILLUSTRATOR'S NOTE

ONCE AGAIN I have been thoroughly captivated by the fertile imagination of Rudyard Kipling and the privilege of bringing my vision to his magical stories in this second volume of a two-volume set. As in Volume 1, each of the stories opens with a sunrise when appropriate. A dominant color permeates each tale, and textures re-appear.

I have used my art to create connections between the stories. Characters and artifacts from one story periodically appear in another. This sometimes means that an object or character from one part of the world appears in another, or that objects from one story may suddenly appear chronologically earlier or later than you might expect. Watch for the leopard butterfly flying through all six tales, as well as other animals from the first volume such as the Elephant's Child and the Camel without his hump.

THE COVER
Landscapes and characters are separated by continents, while the water of rivers and oceans unites them. When a character is transformed, his altered self is shown in a shadow. The cover is divided by a strip of stylized birch bark similar to the bark shown in "How the First Letter Was Written" and "How the Alphabet Was Made," where it forms the background for the illustrations and provides the surface on which the letter and the alphabet are created by Taffy Metallumai and her father.

"THE BEGINNING OF THE ARMADILLOES"
My intent here was to capture the verdant landscape of the "turbid"

Amazon described by Kipling; hence the dominant rainforest greens and the tar black shadows contrast boldly with the pink rock and the luscious turquoise of the river.

The flower shown in the opening illustration is the rare and odoriferous rafflesia, the largest flower in the world, native to the rainforests of the Malay Peninsula, Borneo and Sumatra, not the Amazon rainforest. It is shown here to connect this tale to "The Crab That Played with the Sea" (also set in a verdant landscape), and it can also be found as a tiny drawing on the cave wall in "How the Alphabet Was Made."

"How the First Letter Was Written" and "How the Alphabet Was Made"
In the former tale, Taffy Metallumai writes the first letter on a strip of birch bark for the Stranger-man, and in the latter, her father, Tegumai Bopsulai, creates the alphabet on a strip of bark for the family. Using this element of nature as inspiration, I imagined illustrations drawn and shaded with pencil crayon, pastel pencil and chalk on stylized bark painted with watercolour. The background, therefore, connects the two tales and separates them from the other four. The images here are imbued with more line than is evident in any other story in either volume, giving these two distinctive tales an appropriate drawn effect.

The letters of the alphabet that Tegumai imagines were created by Kipling in the original edition of *Just So Stories* published in 1902. I incorporated Kipling's alphabet to recognize and honour the artist in him within the context of this edition, the past resonating in the present, his alphabet on my birch bark.

Main characters from many of the other stories appear in the pictographs drawn by Taffy and her father on the cave wall before they began to write. You'll also notice the rafflesia previously mentioned, and a mastodon to add historical depth. Taffy's drawings of "The Cat That Walked by Himself" and a "wild thing" (inspired by Maurice Sendak's

Where the Wild Things Are) give the reader an inkling of a young girl's very human dreams while reverberating in the present day. All of these details conspire to create a timeless and literary wall of pictographs, letters, words and stories.

"The Crab That Played with the Sea"

Water plays a critical role in this tropical drama, set on and around an island in the South China Sea. To interpret this aquatic element, the overall effect was created by painting with watercolour on Arches paper, while keeping a light touch with the brush and paint. There are no layers of pigment from other media present, with the exception of three small areas where chalk highlights were employed for dramatic effect.

To ground the image that illustrates the King Crab perched atop the moon to a specific location, I have highlighted the beaches of Pahang, Malaysia, and Sarawak, Borneo, in moonlight, but have also painted the surrounding islands of Sumatra and Sulawesi to broaden the aerial perspective.

"The Cat That Walked by Himself"

For this story, I have employed all four media — watercolour, pencil crayon, pastel pencil and chalk — to evoke the changing atmosphere inside and outside the cave. Watch how they reflect and interpret each scene, and see if you can guess what media is at work and in what areas.

The setting is the ancient Lascaux caves in the Dordogne region of France. The cave images of the horse, stags and hunter are copies of the Paleolithic paintings found on those ancient stone walls. I chose this setting to distinguish this story from the others and to include another continent in this global story collection. Look closer still and you will see the imprints the family left on the wall.

"The Butterfly That Stamped"

At last, after a miraculous journey through twelve of Kipling's best, the intrepid leopard butterfly makes his way home to his wife, as the Mariner in "How the Whale Got His Throat" (Volume 1) makes his way home to his mother, and ultimately a wife. The butterfly is now where he belongs, having reached his own story (so well deserved) in time for it to be told.

Note how lovely his wife is. She is more beautiful than he, in the same way that Balkis is lovelier than her husband, the Most Wise Sovereign Suleiman-bin-Daoud.

To capture the scorching sun of a desert country, I have drawn with pencil crayon and pastel pencil and shaded with chalk on textured paper. A predominance of golds capture Kipling's description of the home of the sovereign and his one thousand wives. Imagine that!

And now we have reached the end. It has been a miraculous and mythic journey. In recognition of my pleasure in illustrating these stories I will be making an annual donation to the International Board on Books for Young People's Children in Crisis Fund. I do this in honour of two IBBY supporters who have also been important to my work over the years — Patsy Aldana and Margaret McElderry (1912–2011), my American editor, who opened the door to this Canadian and changed my professional life forever.

— Ian Wallace

Just So Stories: Volume I
By Rudyard Kipling
Illustrated by Ian Wallace

The first volume of Kipling's classic story collection, with stunning illustrations by Ian Wallace, includes the following:

How the Whale Got His Throat
How the Camel Got His Hump
How the Rhinoceros Got His Skin
How the Leopard Got His Spots
The Elephant's Child
The Sing-Song of Old Man Kangaroo